Dear Carol,

" Life is what hap
As you plan for other things "

Hope you will enjoy the read

June '22

SHIFTING CLOUDS

An anthology of short stories

SHIFTING CLOUDS

An anthology of short stories

Ashoke Mitra

LiFi PUBLICATIONS PVT. LTD.
NEW DELHI

Published by:
LiFi Publications Pvt. Ltd.
211, 2nd Floor, Gagandeep
12, Rajendra Place, New Delhi–110 008, India
Phone : (011) 2574 1000
E-mail : info@lifipublications.com
Web : www.lifipublications.com

ISBN 13: 978-93-82536-70-3   ISBN 10: 93-82536-70-1

First published in 2014

Cataloging in Publication Data—DK
[Courtesy: D.K. Agencies (P) Ltd. <docinfo@dkagencies.com>]

Mitra, Ashoke, 1973–
    Shifting clouds : an anthology of short stories / Ashoke Mitra.
        p.   cm.
    Short stories.
    ISBN 9789382536703

    1. Short stories, Indic (English).   I. Title.

DDC 823.92   23

Printed in India by D.K. Fine Art Press (P) Ltd., Delhi–52.

Contents

Acknowledgement

After having written these short stories in a flow, here I stop fretful and fearful pondering on all those people for whom I could do so, treading carefully so as not to miss anyone. Yet I know there would be names beyond this page that have and would help me be what I am each day. The names mentioned below appear in a random order with no correlation to their degree of help or influence in me or my writing.

I thank my precious and dearest wife, Zinnia who would not go to bed till I read out the story born that day. Her inputs were priceless. I also thank my son Aagneyo and daughter Aabhiri for unknowingly encouraging me to express myself.

My gratefulness goes out to my childhood friend, Tilak Banerjee who has given me very valuable feedback and encouraged me to write. He too is the artist whose sketches accentuate each of my stories and the book cover. Thanks mate, without you this would have been just another run of the mill short story collection.

I also thank my cousin brother Dr. Sayantan Gupta and Dr. Bina Biswas for encouraging me to publish this book.

My eternal gratefulness reaches out to my mom, Pushpita Mitra, who encouraged me to question every aspect of life and believe in the religion of love. I wish she was here to see this day. I wish she is somewhere to see this day.

I thank my two brothers Basudev and Debesh for their valuable inputs.

I also thank my one and only unique uncle Mr. S.P Mitra whose influence in me has been paramount and who has appeared in some form or the other in many of my stories.

Beyond this there are so many friends and relatives across the time zones, all of whom have advertently or inadvertently helped me to complete this book. Thanks all.

Above all thanks to you, the reader without whom my existence would have been meaningless.

Author's Note

'It ends and yet continues beyond' (Shesh hoyia hoyilo na shesh) was how Rabindranath Tagore had described his short stories. Decades have gone by as thousands of short stories been written across the world. Yet, even today I find his simple one liner describing a good short story the best. Short stories have attracted me from the very childhood. Rabindranath, O Henry, Somerset Maugham, Satyajit Ray, Roald Dahl, Ruskin Bond and many more such stalwarts have kept me intrigued in their literary weaving. If novel is a day then short stories would be the seconds, minutes and hours that make it up.

Shifting Clouds is an anthology of short stories capturing a wide range of human emotions and the unpredictable turn of events in life. They will make you cry, laugh, sad, shiver as you ponder on our fundamental belief in God, ghosts, pre-life and after death. Picking up the pen for the first time I have tried to make an honest attempt to touch the deepest corner of the reader's mind. My success awaits judgment in your hands.

1

Octogenarian

I hear a soft knock on the antique mahogany door that has stood the golden test of time like I have. The knock is soft but distinct and demanding; as if someone who owns me is beckoning to open the door. Has she come for me?

As the sound slowly registers in my brain to activate my motor response, I ponder should I even respond? My own tranquilized self asks the question, who am I? Why am I? I smile and say I wish I knew.

If you ever happen to accidentally pick up these few scraps of paper from a forgotten dustbin on some ill-starred day of your life and read, you will not be able to make out who penned down these frivolous thoughts. You won't find my name anywhere. But I know this world cannot do without a name. They need one even when they are hanging someone by the neck. Hanged till death, is what they say.

I am an octogenarian, that's my name. A bit long, odd and too much Latin, I agree but that's the only identity I have standing at this juncture of my life. If you care to look out of your myopic window, a window where you believe you will never ever age, you will see many hapless like me standing at life's crossroads, tired and confused unable to cross the busy street.

My name reminds me of my favorite creature since childhood, a creature of the deep, adapting to all texture and color, suffocating its prey using the eight strong tentacles and yet a loner. I wish I could meet one and look into those inquisitive eyes. I wish I could have shed those eight decades of heavy tentacles trying to choke me to death like an autoimmune disease. So much of memory, so much bitterness, so much to forget and let go.

The knock now has got impatient, I need to answer. As I somehow pick up my dilapidated body, the bones creak, the breathing gets heavier. I drag myself to my antique door to answer.

It's my son, the third one. I have four of them spaced well so as not to have given me much headache as they grew. This one is the softest, most caring and hence the most gullible. Born exactly forty six years ago in the month of July on a rainy Monday afternoon in Kolkata, I even remember the moment I first saw him.

"Yes?"

"Baba, it's me, your son."

"My son? I don't have any sons. I never had any sons. In fact I have never ever married in my life."

"Baba, your dementia is getting worse every day. You are not even recognizing your own kin?"

"No, I don't. But please come in. If you have come to meet me, you must be my well-wisher. Drop in and have a cup of tea."

He walks in with a drooping head, most definitely sad. He has been emotional all his life, taking things too seriously. He still cannot accept the fact that I have burnt the bridge so easily so as not to let him in. It's not just him. I have not acted selectively here. In the last ten years I have very methodically burnt down all the bridges one by one. This one which my sons used was the most difficult of them all, so I had to keep it for the last.

They say I have age related amnesia, a natural degradation of the memory cells so as to wipe out your past each growing day. How I wish it was true! How I wish my brain cells had betrayed me to help me live like a clean slate. But alas! That is not the case. So I had to take matters in my own hand. I created my own disease just like I had proudly created my world of bricks mortars and steel all my life.

It all started a decade back when my beautiful and elegant wife left me. I am not sure where she went. They all say it was painful but I say it was a relief. I could almost hear her sigh of redemption as she left. Tranquility, she could have only got by severing all ties with me. She made me realize that day what a pathetic failure I was in life. Famous, rich, intelligent, riding on luck and touching the pinnacle of glory, I was at the end of the day a lone King, guarding his abandoned empire.

It was not that I never cared for her or my sons. I loved them all. But I loved myself more than any of them. Flying in my own momentum in the predestined trajectory, I was too full of myself to take care of anything else. She took it all on her. I am thankful not to find a trace of my shadow on any of them four. How clinically she removed ebony from ivory. And what did I give her in return? Misery, misery and more misery. So help me God.

The day she gave me a jolt and went away, I realized her worth. I realized what she meant to me and how psychologically dependent I was on her. One fine morning she created a void in my life which I had no clue how to fill. I wanted to make it up to her, but it was too late. Remorse and penitence kept me awake all night. I roamed about in the house searching every nook and corner for my amputated self, hoping it would be my heart that I will discover below the sofa someday. I never found it, maybe I never had one. My sympathetic sons called the doctor. Shock... he commented. Senility settling in was his prognosis.

I tried hard to change myself, thinking I would make it up to my sons in a way could not do to her. But every person I would meet would only talk about her. They would sing about her magnanimity, her golden heart, her tolerance and selfless deeds. All of them spoke without a hint of fib, I knew. But it all came and mocked me and made me realize how worthless I was. I couldn't take it and hence decided to disconnect myself by and by. It was a difficult road to traverse, but that was the only way out for me.

Have I been successful in unhooking myself from my eight decades with clinical precision? I don't think so. Slips happen every now and then.

My youngest is settled outside. He comes to visit me with his family once in a while. Last time he came, he was concerned. My selfish act of destruction had already started. As he walked in holding his sons hand after having traveled across the world, expecting a hint of remembrance from me, I once thought I should. I thought let me once rise beyond being just me and do it for someone else. But the moment I looked at his face I was petrified. Even with my cataract affected murky eyes I could see the magical resemblance between him and her. Yes, I remember, she would say, "My youngest is my prototype." I had never bothered to look closely, who had the time for such frivolous acts? But there he was, smiling from his heart. But all I could see was her sarcastic smile. I cut the last desperate link to the bridge. He was sad. Let him be.

But when his four year old son held my hand and asked me, "Dadu, how are you?" I forgot all my terms and conditions. I held his hand, called him by his name and asked him a few questions, immaculate, precise and accurate, a fatal slip in my model, a weak point in my fortress. They were all surprised. No one could explain how, neither could I.

The other slip that happens is when I meet my brother. He comes to me with a smell of the only decade I still want to remember, the first one. That is the only tentacle that is still free, that is the only one which leaves me alone. Childhood nostalgia is what they say. Come what may, that part of the memory is never erased!

This is all I have today to pen down. Years and years of relentless struggle to achieve the glorious limelight, decades of persistent effort to bask in the glory, millions of praises, awards and handshakes all boiled down to these few pages of scribble. Born a narcissistic I am and will die the same....

I again hear a soft knock on the antique mahogany door that has stood the golden test of time like I have. The knock is soft but distinct and demanding; as if someone who owns me is beckoning to open the door.

Has she finally come for me?

✦ ✦ ✦

2

Fame

I

Ratan Das, a student, in a government school in West Bengal was a back bencher. No one could say whether he chose the bench or the bench chose him. Whatever be the reason, they looked at perfect harmony with each other. For Ratan it helped him stay as far away from the teacher as possible while for the bench, it was glad to have a constant companion.

It's not that he hated studies. On the contrary, he was quite eager to study and learn new things in the class. Unfortunately, his brain could not fathom the esoteric teachings in the classroom. What was lectured sounded Hebrew, what was written looked Latin. When he tried to answer any question asked by the teacher or was called to the black board to solve any mathematical problems, it seemed a boy from the lower class had mistakenly entered a higher one. Due to his slow understanding, he had to be kept back in each class for more than a year. All his fellow classmates would gleefully move on to the upper class at the end of the term as he would sit despondent at one corner, waiting to welcome the new faces swarm in. He was a source of entertainment for the other kids as they would pull his leg and joke about him being an idiot.

Had it been a recognized public school somewhere in the city, he would have been asked to leave many years back. But life in the villages is much laid back, compared to the hustle bustle of the city. Moreover, this was a government school and the attitude and approach towards the students was much lenient.

Ratan's father, an illiterate poor farmer always tried his level best to make ends meet. All he knew was that he had to fulfill his duty of sending his only son to school, a duty he considered essential to ensure his son not suffering the same fate as his.... Beyond that he had no clue. So when the teachers had called him once to give him feedback about his son, his closely clasped hands, bent back and blank look made them instantly realize they had wasted their time.

And so, Ratan continued his journey in the school at a snail's pace, forcefully being moved up a class every two to three years. The teachers and the students had accepted him as part of the school just like the huge banyan tree at the corner of the playground, standing relentlessly with no expectation from the world. As he tried to adjust his legs in the smaller benches and look around at all the new faces at the beginning of the year, Ratan would often contemplate quitting. He thought he should accept his intellectually stunted self and go back to the real world and help his dad. He would have done so had it not been for Manoj.

Manoj, yet again belonging to a poor agricultural background was a prodigious child. He had exhibited his amazing intelligence at the age of three as he started solving mathematical problems meant for the fifth grade. Be it science or literature he was always ahead of his age. The teachers knew that this lad had immense potential and would make them proud one day.

Ratan first met Manoj when he was stranded in class four for two consecutive years. The old batch had moved on as Manoj walked in one fine morning in the class with a breath of fresh air and suppressed expectation. They both were already famous in the school for their own reasons.

To Ratan's surprise, Manoj came and sat next to him. He held out his hand towards Ratan with a simple smile and said, "Hi, I am Manoj. You are Ratan, right?"

"Yea, I am. But don't you think you should be sitting on the front bench? You might spoil your reputation. No one sits here. This bench is for stupid students like me who are stuck in the same class for decades."

Manoj laughed aloud and said, "Is it? Who says so? Is it because the old teachers teach at a very low decibel? Or is it that the teachings are absorbed by the front and middle students in the class and what reaches the back is void?"

Ratan was pleasantly touched by the sanguine and humble gesture of the prodigy. Thus began that day a unique friendship beyond the peripheries of rational understanding. The apparently unbridgeable gap of age and intellect posed no challenge to their bond.

Manoj, with the heavy cloud of expectation looming over his head, found a solace when with Ratan. He saw in his eyes an immediate acceptance for what he was and not what he might be.

Ratan, with the dark cloud of disappointment looming over his head, also found a solace when with Manoj. He saw in his eyes an immediate acceptance for what he was and not what he ever would fail to be. He started loving him and felt possessive about him like his own younger brother. Manoj was progressing like a rocket already ignited and launched in its path, focused with full energy and power. Ratan sat at the launching site, looking at his distant friend with proud and reverent eyes. There was no way they could have run at the same pace. Hence, at the end of that year, Manoj exited the class as Ratan stayed back yet again. But this never affected their bond. The four walls of the classroom were too small a boundary for them. They would walk back and forth to school together sharing their own dreams without hesitation.

"You know Ratan, my dream is to become a doctor one day. A cardio specialist who would save thousands of lives, someone people would love and worship at the same time. My fame should travel beyond any religious, political or demographic boundaries. I want to be famous." Manoj would confide while swaying back from school.

"What about you? What is your dream? What do you want to become one day?" he would ask Ratan with utmost simplicity.

Ratan would smile and answer, "I don't have a dream Manoj. I don't think I am allowed to have one. All I know is that education will never help me earn my bread. I need to survive. That is my dream."

Thus, the years rolled by with one galloping and the other crawling as the friendship got stronger each day. Ratan knew deep within that this ephemeral journey would end one day and so it did.

By the time Manoj passed his board exam, he had exhibited such brilliance that his parents decided to give him a better opportunity. He had an uncle working in Delhi, and his whole family decided to relocate to provide him with schools and colleges which would do justice to the talent.

On the last day as Manoj's parents sat inside the train anxiously waiting for him to board, he held Ratan's hand and said, "I will miss you. But we will be in touch. I will write a letter to you as soon as I reach the capital."

Ratan didn't say anything. He just pressed Manoj's hand gently and handed him a piece of paper. It was a sketch of two little boys walking hand in hand on an empty village road, looking ahead towards the horizon where the mud road abruptly vanished.

Manoj's eyes got moist. "You sketch so well Ratan, I never knew!"

"It's just a token of the time we spent, a gift I could afford Manoj.... May you achieve your dream one day."

Not even once did Ratan mention, "We will meet again, or see you soon or we will be in touch." As the train gradually left the platform, Ratan stood there till the tail vanished into the unknown. Heaving a sigh he started walking back home.

Ratan never went back to the school. He had no reason to. His life changed drastically in the next few years. His only other emotional link to this world, his dad, whom he had started helping in the field, suddenly left him. It was a mysterious disease beyond the knowledge of the village quacks. After his father's demise Ratan realized the land they had been tilling was not even their own. With everything gone he had no other option but to move to Kolkata in search for a job.

II

Fifteen grueling years went by since Ratan left his village. Kolkata and her people were never kind to him. He had to fight for his existence each day. He had tried his hands on everything to survive. However, last three years of life seemed to have a little less turmoil as he worked for a newspaper agency. It was a famous newspaper company, Kolkata Times and he had got the job of a peon there. His job was to run errands for anybody and everybody in the office starting from getting a cup of tea, running down the street to get a packet of cigarettes or distributing the couriers and letters to designated desks. In spite of the rough road life had laid down for him, his simplicity never left him. He was still the back bencher, watching the world flow by with no expectation from anyone.

People in this office liked him a lot. He was always there when they needed him. He himself was also happy to have finally got a place to work where he was referred by his name and not just a 'hey'. Finally he had an entity, however small it was.

It happened on a Wednesday afternoon. As he was trying to hastily cross the street to reach the pan shop for a pack of cigarette, a motorcycle hit him at full speed. The momentum threw him off his feet as he went and hit the lamp post. There was a dead silence for a few seconds as people thought it was all over for him. But immediately the crowd regained their senses and rushed to his aid. He was lying on the floor unconscious, bleeding heavily from his head, but was breathing. His office people called for an ambulance and took him to a nearby hospital straight into the ICU.

"How is he, doctor?" Asked Meenakshi, an employee in the same newspaper agency Ratan ran errands for. Meenakshi, an attractive, young and fiercely independent lady was the chief editor. She had always liked Ratan and had rushed with the entire team to the hospital. She had been waiting there all along the two hours of surgery.

"Difficult to say, Ma'am. His bleeding has stopped though. He was badly hit on his left eye. Let's wait for twenty four hours and observe. But even if he gets back to his senses I doubt his vision will get back to normal." Replied the doctor.

To everyone's relief Ratan came back to consciousness the next day. His head and left eye were still heavily bandaged as he was moved to the normal ward.

"Didi, so much expense!" were the first words he mumbled as Meenakshi came to visit him the next day.

"You don't worry Ratan. We will all contribute and take care of that. You get well soon."

Ratan was touched. He started weeping through his right eye as he thanked her. After fifteen years of being shunned from one corner of Kolkata to the other and treated like reprocessed garbage, he had forgotten that the world could also be kind.

Least did he suspect there was a drastic change that had taken place in him. A change he could have never ever imagined. A change he would get to know in three days' time.

"I am going to run some simple tests here Ratan to ensure you are fine. Is that OK?" Asked the doctor as he gradually opened Ratan's dressing.

"Can you gradually come down from the bed and walk on this white line?" requested the doctor.

Ratan was a bit groggy, but could walk on the line without faltering.

"Good," said the doctor.

"Now, look straight at me. Close your right eye and try to see my hand using your left. What do you see?" the doctor held out his right hand with an open palm.

"A dark patch doctor. As if I am viewing the world through a key hole. I can't see clearly," replied Ratan nervously.

"Hmm. Okay now do the opposite. Close your left and try and see with your right."

"Now I can see you and your hand clearly, doctor," exclaimed Ratan.

"Okay, now open both your eyes and try to see."

"Doctor, there is a pigeon on your head!" screamed Ratan.

"What?" shouted the doctor as he almost jumped back trying to shoo away the imaginary pigeon from over his head using his hand!

"What are you saying?" shouted the doctor, now embarrassed at his own behavior. The nurses in the room could hardly control their laughter.

"That's right, Doctor, I clearly saw it. But now that you jumped it's gone!"

"OK, okay. Maybe you are still to recover from the shock. Well, Ratan it seems your left eye vision has been partially affected. You should consider yourself lucky going by the way you were hit. I will give you few medicines and some exercises. We will see how it goes. Many a times, people recover after a while. As for your going home, I think you can be discharged tomorrow."

Next day Meenakshi along with some more office colleagues went through the discharge formalities. She made him sit in a taxi, gave him some money and said, "Take care Ratan. I have spoken to our boss. You can take two weeks off. Get well and join back office. We need you fast, who will do the running around for us?" said Meenakshi jovially.

"Thanks Didi. I will never forget what you all have done for me," said Ratan as the taxi just started to move. But just as it had moved a few feet, he screamed and asked the driver to stop. "Didi, there is a lizard on your shoulder!"

"What??" shouted Meenakshi at the top of her voice and stood there petrified, eyes closed. Hearing her scream one of her fellow colleague came running to her help.

"What's wrong Meenakshi. Why are you screaming?"

"Partha, Ratan has seen a lizard on my shoulder. Quickly do something." Her eyes were still closed.

"Meenakshi, there is nothing on you. Open your eyes."

To this Meenakshi opened her eyes to check her sari and heaved a sigh of relief.

"What kind of practical joke was that Ratan? Scaring me out of my wits? You think it's funny? This is your way of saying thank you after all we have done for you?" she was furious.

"I swear Didi, I saw one," sheepishly replied Ratan.

"Enough, I think the accident has affected your mind. Go home, take some rest and come back sane."

With this Meenakshi turned back and walked away as the taxi driver started to drive slowly through the Kolkata traffic. Ratan was perplexed. He did not understand what was happening to him. First it was the pigeon and now the lizard. He could swear on anything living or dead that he had seen them. He was surprised to realize each time that it was just him.

As the days progressed and his body started to heal, something in his brain didn't. Those weird characters started appearing in his vision every now and then. It could be as funny as a piglet hanging from the tree by its tiny tail or as scary as a red eyed monster staring down at him in the middle of the night. They could come up anytime of the day, under any circumstances, anywhere, random. Ratan was alarmed and terrified to start with. He thought the accident had made some permanent damage to his brain and he had gone insane. Bachelor and a loner Ratan never had many friends with whom he could have shared this. Moreover, after how the doctor and Meenakshi had reacted, he was skeptical to talk about this to anyone. There was another peculiarity that he noticed in his illusions. They were all two dimensional cartoon characters and would gel perfectly with reality.

Maybe they were figment of his imagination gone wild. Maybe he had gone partially insane. Maybe they were his innermost self, trying to befriend him. He did not know. It was well beyond him to comprehend the change, but it was well within him to accept his distorted self without any remorse or despondence. That's how he had survived all these years. When he realized these imaginary characters were reflections of his own mind and they meant no harm, he befriended them. His otherwise boring mundane life brightened up in a flash. It was as if during the surgery the doctor had forgotten a magnifying glass inside his brain as his power of imagination multiplied many folds. The dowdy lady with a passive face walking past his house every morning looked like a decked up bull dog, a black cat would roll across the street through a moving bus and stand on the other side grinning at him, a pink buffalo would peep through his window with a smiling face, a scarlet crow would sit on a garbage bin and caw to draw his attention. It was as if someone had picked up the brush and painted Kolkata's ever grey and polluted canvas with resplendent colors.

When Ratan joined office after two weeks, with a slight limp on his right leg, he was mentally rejuvenated. He was much more jovial and was happy to be back amongst people whom he knew cared for him.

"How are you doing Ratan?" asked Meenakshi as he went to her table with a cup of tea.

"I am doing fine Didi. Thanks for all you have done and sorry for that day," he apologized.

"You should let that sleep and continue working the way you had been. By the way, it was just not me. The entire office contributed to help you out." Clarified Meenakshi.

So Ratan jumped back into the rhythm as if he had never missed a beat, ready at everyone's beck and call, running all day, not bothering to take rest till the last employee would leave the office. No one noticed the change except Ratan, who had his myriad colorful friends assisting him all day.

It was a Friday. Already in the weekend mood, people had left office a bit early. Ratan decided to clean the conference room before shutting down the office and calling it a day. As he entered the room he found all the chairs in disarray, coffee cups and mugs all lying on the table, uneaten pizza, biscuits and chips on the plates. He sighed. This would take some time. He picked up the tray and started putting the cups on it when his glance fell on the white board. Beyond a few gibberish scribbles the board had been wiped clean. The different colored markers were lying on the table, waiting to be picked up. After decades Ratan felt an inexorable desire to sketch something. He hesitated. He was not supposed to use the white board. If someone would get to know he would lose his job. But it was an empty office. Who would get to know? Anyway, he would rub it off before leaving the room.

Ratan picked up the markers and started to draw on the long white board. What followed was an ecstatic outburst of colors and characters in all shape size and form. It was as if Van Gogh and Picasso had returned from their graves. Ratan had always loved to sketch and draw when he was a child. Life's hostile twist and turns had inundated his desire. But now with his imagination heightened, he could not stop himself from drawing the characters. He drew as he saw, a seamless mix of reality and surrealism, people whom he knew from this world as caricature with his friends from the other world.

He had no idea how much time had lapsed. He was lost in his world.

"Ratan?"

Ratan was shocked and jumped back.

Meenakshi was standing at the door with an expression of quizzical surprise on her face. She had come back to pick up something she had forgotten.

"What are you doing?"

"Didi, I am sorry. I know I should not have. Please forgive me. I will rub it off right now," pleaded a nervous Ratan as he picked up the duster and hurriedly tried to erase his creation.

"Stop, just stop," shouted Meenakshi as she gazed at the white board in bewilderment.

"This is marvelous Ratan. How could you draw like this?"

Ratan was still standing next to the board, frozen with his hands in the air, about to wipe the characters, afraid and embarrassed.

"I don't know Didi. I just draw whatever I see," he timidly replied.

"This is fantastic. You have a talent my friend. What are you doing running from table to table trying to meet our frivolous demands? Don't wipe this. I want everyone to see this on Monday. Do you understand?"

Ratan nodded.

"Good. I am leaving. Lock the office and leave once you are done. We will talk on Monday."

To Ratan's discomfiture everyone started to praise him on Monday. The board room acted like an art gallery in the museum as people would walk by to appreciate the work of art displayed.

"I have an idea, Bhaskar," Meenakshi was in the room of the Managing Director, Bhaskar Bose.

"What is it Meenakshi?" Bhaskar incredulously looked up from his laptop.

"You have seen Ratan 's sketches and you yourself admitted they are unique. Why don't we use it to our benefit? Why can't we have a column where his sketches would come out depicting the issue of the day? The way he looks at things I am sure it would give a funny and different perspective to the news. This world gets bored very soon Bhaskar. Every news channel or paper broadcast the same news. But we have an opportunity of dressing it up differently." Conveyed Meenakshi passionately.

"Hmm, you have a point there for sure. But Meenakshi, this guy might have imagination and a master stroke, but he is quite dumb. How can you expect him to understand the criticality of the news and make a caricature out of it?"

"I have thought about that. Leave that to me. I will have someone explain the news we want to highlight to him and let his pen and imagination flow."

"Well, I am open to the idea. Give it a shot. I think it's worth a try," encouraged Bhaskar.

What followed in the weeks to come was an unexpected turn of events for Ratan. His unique way of depicting the news of the day was merrily accepted by the people of Kolkata. Tired of this dark world and its repetitive news, his humor was a welcome change for all. He was made a permanent employee and was given a corner desk to sit and draw. A small boy replaced him running from table to table and embarrassing him every once in a while with a cup of tea.

III

Manoj's trajectory had not slowed down. He continued passing all the exams with flying colors to get admission in MBBS. There also he topped and did his specialization in cardio. He was now settled in Kolkata, attached to a very famous hospital. He was a well-known cardio surgeon, revered in his fraternity for having achieved such a status so early in life.

The cartoons, caricatures and sketches in Kolkata Times had caught his attention when it first started five years back. Like everyone else, he was intrigued and looked forward to the next day's hilarious representations. The sign RD in one corner of the picture had made his mind pause for a second. But then he ignored the impossible. But that day when Ratan received the best cartoonist of the year award from the chief minister of Bengal and he saw that on TV, he got curious. The middle aged man with grey hair and broken cheeks walking the stage with a slight limp to receive the award aroused his suspicion. Then when the camera zoomed into his smiling face, Manoj jumped out of his seat in amazement and euphoria.

Finding Ratan's address was the easiest part as one of his patients worked for Kolkata Times.

The person who answered the door as Manoj rang the bell of a small flat in Beadon street, North Kolkata, had drastically aged. But Manoj had no problem in identifying his childhood friend. He could not speak as he stood there trembling in excitement. Ratan stood there looking at Manoj, expectant. There was no way he could have recognized the bald headed, potbellied metamorphosed Manoj after so many years.

"Ratan, it's me, Manoj."

Ratan could not believe his eyes. He was overwhelmed. They hugged each other and did not speak for a while. After overcoming the pleasant shock, they sat down on the sofa, still trying to believe that they had found each other.

"Let me make a cup of tea for you Manoj."

"Don't bother, sit. We have so much to talk."

"You keep on talking Manoj. I don't have a mansion. My kitchen is right here at the corner of the room. So tell me, how are you, what are you, where are you? Tell me everything."

As Manoj walked around the room appreciating the multiple sketches all across the wall narrating his success story, Ratan felt proud. He was amazed to realize that he still had that brotherly feeling for him.

"So, you tell me Ratan. How did you catapult to this fame? I did see one sketch of yours and I still have it, but these are brilliant. It's as if you have been transported to a surreal world where only you have an access. I even see you have started working for a full-fledged Bollywood animation film!"

"It's nothing of that sort Manoj. God has been kind to me. I had been struggling to survive, as expected. But then something happened in my life which changed everything. Something I have never ever shared with anyone."

Manoj was as attentive as ever. "What?"

"I met with an accident Manoj about five years back. A two wheeler hit me hard and I injured my head critically. Thanks to God and the people in my office, I survived. But I never got back the normal vision in my left eye. But the most surprising part was since then I have been seeing imaginary cartoon characters all around me as if they are part of my own world. Psyched to start with I accepted my fate and started drawing whatever I would see. That is what you see in my sketches. Apparently from another world, they are nothing but mine. You are a doctor. Tell me, do you think I have gone insane?"

Manoj was transported to a different time frame deep within his dormant memory. His MBBS class in neuro biology. Professor P. Banerjee was delivering his lectures in his absorbing signature style:

"Sometimes people with significant visual loss, have vivid, complex recurrent visual hallucinations. One characteristic of these hallucinations is that they are usually Lilliputian. The most common hallucination is of faces or cartoons. The sufferer understands that the hallucinations are only visual and not occurring in any other senses like hearing, smell or taste."

Named after the Swiss naturalist who had first detected this abnormal behavior in his own eighty nine year old grandfather in 1769, Ratan was unarguably suffering from Charles Bonnet syndrome.

Manoj got up and hugged Ratan once again.

"If you are insane Ratan then let the whole world be like you."

Born a prodigy, destined to be successful, Manoj touched a thousand hearts to give them hope to live. Yet his fame had not traveled beyond the boundaries of Kolkata.

Born an idiot, destined to be doomed, Ratan had touched millions of hearts beyond any boundaries to give them happiness to live.

The half-witted boy sitting idly at the launching site gazing at the distant rocket had unexpectedly overtaken....

✦ ✦ ✦

3

Parsimony

I

It was a dream coming true for Deepak as he got commissioned from the Indian Military Academy. Marching in perfect harmony to the tune of Auld Lang Syne with his fellow cadets, he could see his dad and fiancée Puja sitting proudly in the stand. He had waited for this day since childhood, a day when he would get to serve his country. A bright and sunny day in Dehradun, it could not have been a better setting as the black stars of a Rifle Regiment shone on Deepak's shoulder. With a sense of pride, he felt he had crossed that thin line, to enter a different world, a world where everyone held on to their titles more than their names, where discipline was as basic as breathing and a preordained caste system, meant for better efficiency and not insult, existed to everyone's tacit understanding.

"So Lt. Deepak Arora, how does it feel?" Puja was leaning against the door, happy and relaxed observing Deepak as he entered the guest house in the evening.

Deepak touched his father's feet before smiling at Puja and lying down on the sofa. He felt extremely light and relaxed.

"So, where is Gorkha Regiment at present?" asked his dad.

"They are located in Jaipur presently." proudly announced Deepak.

"Wow, that's great son. I am sure you would know that Gorkha Regiments have been part of the Indian Army since the time of the British. Six of the regiments were transferred to Indian Army post independence. These Gorkhas are primarily from Nepal and are very loyal and fierce fighters. In fact the British Army, even today, has a regiment known as Royal Gurkha Rifles where they continue to recruit from Nepal. It is an honor son, to know you are now part of that league." Deepak's dad was excited like a child. He had never ever served the army. In fact no one in their distant relation was part of Indian Army. Yet, his dad's know-how was amazing.

"So you would be posted out of Jaipur now?" Puja was anxious.

"Well, yes and it seems I would be stationed there for at least two more years. I am expected to join duty in two months' time."

"Wonderful," shouted his dad. "Then you two should get married next month itself so that she can go with you as you join duty."

Deepak and Puja knew each other since they were ten years old. Next door neighbors in Sarojini Nagar, South Delhi, they grew up as very close friends. There was nothing in each other's lives that they would not share. They walked into each other's houses as if those were their own. So when Deepak proposed to her three years back, she was a bit perplexed and confused. She was unsure whether such a camaraderie could be transferred successfully to a nuptial bond. She took some time to think and Deepak never forced. He knew that he would be the winner and he was.

They had a civil marriage. No ceremony, no pandemonium, no white mare trying desperately to reach the marriage site to unload her burden and take some respite from the deafening sound, no fat uncles and aunts dancing (as if that evening was their last). It was a very atypical Panjabi marriage, usually known for its pomp, glory and display of wealth. All of Deepak's relatives were unhappy and insisted to have a proper one. But Deepak was adamant. He never wanted to waste money on such silly social obligations.

"Are you two sure? I am getting lot of pressure from everyone." Deepak's dad wanted to know before the marriage.

"Hundred percent dad. How much had you planned to throw away?"

"Well, I had kept aside ten lakhs for this, hoping it would be enough. But now since you two have decided this way, I will make a Fixed Deposit and hand it over to you."

"Bravo!" shouted Deepak.

Deepak from his early childhood was very judicious with money. Whatever pocket money he would get while going to school, he would spend the minimal and save the rest. While his friends would derive immense pleasure out of the road side, unhygienic, cheap food, he would convince himself of the health hazard and put the money in the piggy bank. Saving money, he realized, gave him more satisfaction than spending it. If asked he would say, "I am planning for the future." However, beyond that he had no answer. As he grew older, this nature became a habit to such an extent that he was nicknamed Uncle Scrooge by his friends.

Puja obviously was aware of this trait of Deepak's. It's not that she never got bothered or irritated. Yet, she accepted this in him and decided to test the relationship till death would do them apart, due to two reasons. First, she knew no one in this world could be perfect. Deepak as a person was very considerate and mature. He was jovial and optimistic about life and supported her whenever required. What else could she have asked for? Second, deep within she hoped and believed he will change post marriage. That her dramatically opposite approach of living and enjoying the present would gradually influence and change him.

With this buoyant expectation she held Deepak's hand as he firmly held the Fixed Deposit, to walk into their new life.

"Where are we going for honeymoon?" inquired Puja just as they came out of the court.

"As I told you before darling, it is a surprise! You will get to know tomorrow as we board the train."

"Train? Deepak where are we going? I thought you will be taking me to a foreign country!" exclaimed Puja.

Deepak's face grew dark. He knew he had got into a tight corner and had to wriggle himself out.

"Puja dear, we are going to Goa. The heaven for honeymoon couples. I am telling you, you won't regret it," tried to convince Deepak.

"Goa? That too by train?" Puja was almost in tears.

"It is the best way to commute Puja, safe and eco-friendly. Also come to think how romantic it would be."

"I can't believe this. All my friends have gone to foreign countries for their honeymoon. They were all asking me, as I told them it's a surprise. You know what they said? Uncle Scrooge's surprise? Well has to be interesting. I ignored their sarcasm with the only hope that you would not disappoint me this time. But it was my mistake. You can never grow beyond your stinginess Deepak, not even for me!"

"Puja please, don't make a scene here. Believe me, this was the best I could afford. You know I haven't even got my first salary yet!"

"What about the money dad gave you?" asked Puja.

"That's for the future Puja."

"You and your future! I don't know what to say."

"Please Puja, let's not start our life's journey on this note. Trust me; I will take you for a foreign trip one day."

"Promise?" Puja looked into his eyes.

"Promise." Deepak hurriedly said looking away. He had seen a ray of hope. He had to exit the quagmire immediately.

Puja also never wanted to have a fight to start their life. So she made herself believe that Deepak was being truthful and decided to accept the flow of tide.

Notwithstanding the jumpy start, their conjugal life went well in the months to come. When they arrived at Jaipur, it was the onset of winter. Rajasthan during the winter was a perfect backdrop for them to start a quiet and passionate life.

On one such passionate night as they were lying next to each other, Puja observed a locket hanging from Deepak's neck. It was a small and sharp object made out of brass delicately put through a silver chain.

"What's this?" whispered Puja surprised.

"It's a bullet, Darling, yet to be fired," announced Deepak proudly.

Puja was shocked. "Why are you wearing it?"

Deepak smiled. "In Army we believe, there is a bullet designed and destined to take each of our lives. We also believe that wearing it you cheat death and change your destiny." Puja's eyes got moist. She hugged and kissed Deepak, "Let's not talk about death. Nothing will ever happen to you. You will be with me forever."

The Army life though, came and hit Puja as a big change. It was a microcosm where each day and move was predictable and planned. Puja by nature had always been opposite. Planning for things had never been her forte. So it took her a while to get adjusted to the new environment. Whenever and wherever she would meet with the officer's wives, nothing other than army life would be discussed. The hierarchy was more evident amongst them rather than their uniformed husbands. Puja felt claustrophobic at times, yearning to breathe. To start with, she always had Deepak to come back to where she could have a varied discussion. But as years went by she observed a drastic change in him too. It was as if there existed a clandestine centrifugal force which would insidiously pull away people from their civilian existence. With a sigh, she accepted her world like a bird would accept her clipped wing.

Deepak, on the other hand did very well in his profession. It was as if he was born to be part of this. His energy, exuberance and passionate patriotism catapulted him into the limelight. By the time he was promoted as a Major his uniform had become significantly heavier with the medals. But what had grown heavier still was his pride and ego. Even after ten years he was still extremely agile and fit, unlike most of his colleagues at the same rank, and would give the young Lieutenants a run for their money. He was also an outstanding marksman. Kalashnikovs, carbines, self-loading rifles, LMG or pistols he would always hit the bulls eye. As he would come back from the shooting range all charged up and euphoric, Puja would ask, "You must have again got all the bull's eye, looking at your face."

"Yes, yes and yes. You know what, they are even considering me to represent the national team." Deepak was boisterous.

"That's really good. But I still fail to understand how can you get so much pleasure out of something designed to take away someone's life? One look at those objects makes me sad."

"It is matter of perspective dear. If I don't kill they will. My hands itch for the real situation when I could prove my point." clarified Deepak.

"You can kill someone in cold blood?" Puja was horrified.

"Of course I can, point blank, looking straight into his eyes." replied Deepak nonchalantly.

Puja looked into Deepak's eyes and tried to search her childhood friend and young lover. Someone had taken him away. The humble, jovial and resplendent butterfly had retro-metamorphosed in the last ten years.

But one trait remained unaltered. Rather, was amplified. It was his miserliness. He would try to cut every corner to save money. Whenever Puja would ask for a gift he would have some excuse. After a while she stopped asking out of insult. Other than going back to Delhi, they never went out anywhere else for their holidays. Thus grew his bank balance. Thus grew her sadness. A child could have brought her a draft of cold breeze. But Deepak was not keen. "I am not ready to take the responsibility yet." he would say. But deep within her she knew the real reason.

The movement order of the battalion to an area named Poonch, in the southern lap of the mighty Pirpanjal, bordering Pakistan, came as no surprise to Deepak. He had got to know from his sources well in advance that this time it would be one of the sensitive posts. Tension between the two countries had heightened post the Kargil War. As the politicians tried to solve for the imminent danger from their far away comfortable chairs, it seemed Pakistan was surreptitiously sending highly skilled and trained people across the border to carry out terrorist activities in India. Indian army had to be vigilant day and night to prevent such infiltrations. They would give their life but let someone pass through.

Deepak was shivering with excitement. He had finally got his chance to serve his country at the border, an opportunity where he could confront his enemy in flesh and blood. Puja was worried but knew that she had no other option but to hope for the best and wait till eternity for his safe return. She went back to Delhi while Major Deepak Arora, ordered his troop to move with full gusto.

II

Sher Khan was completely submerged in his morning prayers in an isolated small cottage up in the mountains of Swat Valley, Pakistan. On the floor next to him lay two of his most trusted companions in life, companions without whom he would not travel anywhere, companions whom he cared for and trusted more than his own wife and children. One was the Holy Quran, a miniature version which was convenient to carry anywhere. The other was his AK-47 rifle. A selective-fire, gas-operated 7.62 mm assault rifle, first developed in the Soviet Union by Mikhail Kalashnikov, this was with him since he fought the Russians in Afghanistan. Light, accurate and reliable – it had never betrayed him. Standing at six feet six inches, fashioning a beard which ran beyond his neck and with a scar running from below his left eye till his right chin, Sher Khan was an ominous *Mujahedeen*. The word Mujahedeen in Arabic meant people doing Jihad or Muslims struggling in the path of Allah to protect Islam. Sher Khan was a pure Mujahedeen who could go out of the way to fight for his religion. The scar on his face bore testimony to that. But he never believed in meaningless terrorist attacks, suicide bombings and killing innocent people not linked to Jihad. This was a sole reason for which post the Russians left Afghanistan, he could never work with his team and decided to operate alone.

"*Sabah el kheer*, Sher Khan."

Two tall *Pathans* had been waiting outside the door for Sher Khan to finish his prayers. They knew him too well to disturb him during his prayers.

"*Sabah el kheer, marhaban*," greeted back Sher Khan and asked them to come in.

As they sat down on the floor, Sher Khan looked at them with an impassive expression. He was a man of very few words and expected people interacting with him also to stick to that rule.

"Yes, of course, we will come to the point." hurriedly expressed one of the Pathans, getting the hint.

"This time it's a big mission, Khan. There is a handover taking place between the Gorkha and the Rajputana Rifles. You have to go in and finish off a significant few."

"Where?" Sher Khan had no emotion in his voice.

"Poonch," replied the Pathans.

"Price?" asked Sher Khan.

"You name the price Khan. This has come from the top and money is no bar." assured the Pathans.

"Two lakhs for each head and five for an officer, three lakhs now and the rest on successful completion of the mission." Sher Khan was very particular when it came to negotiations and transactions.

"There you go, five lakhs here." They had come prepared and put down a sling bag in front of him.

"OK, Sher Khan. In a month's time my men will drop you near the border. Beyond that it will be just you."

As the guests left, Sher Khan looked at the bag lying in front of him and smiled. Deep within he was tired of leading this nomadic life, deeper within he was tired of killing. He wanted to now settle down with his family and lead the life of an average peasant. This assignment would give him enough money to lead a peaceful life. Price per head was what he had demanded and price per head was what he had been assured. He had to ensure maximum kill.

"You need to be extra vigilant Major," cautioned Lt. Col P. K. Gupta as he was debriefing Deepak on the terrain. "You see, they are always looking for an opportunity to sneak through the fences. Indian Government has spent millions of rupees to secure the border, yet it is not hundred percent foolproof and that's where our job becomes so critical. These are Mujahedeen, trained to dissolve in this terrain and kill without blinking an eye. They get assignments on some terrorist attack in some part of the country for which they would sneak in. Historically we have observed that whenever there is a change of hands in these posts, the infiltration rate goes up. So you need to have extra patrols planned for the initial three four months till you all are well acclimatized with this area."

"Yes Sir," was all that came out as a shout from excited Deepak.

The handover was spread out for the next one month after which the Rajputana soldiers left the post and it was left completely to the Gorkha to protect the border.

Poonch's terrain was extremely treacherous. Situated at an altitude above six thousand feet, the entire border was covered in dense coniferous jungle with deep crevasses in between. There was no way to ensure the safety of the Line of Control without having a regular patrol scanning the entire area at least twice a day. It was a bone breaking task, to patrol an area like that, as about ten to twelve Gorkha would make a file and travel through the dense jungle heavily armed. Not many army officers in the rank of a Major would be part of these patrols as it would mostly be taken care of by the Lieutenants, Captains and the Junior Commissioned Officer more popularly known as JCOs. But Deepak was an exception. He would not only be part of the daily patrols but lead it from the front.

Sher Khan arrived at the border in the evening, dressed up in a dark green pathani suit carrying his two trusted friends. He would be helped by the locals to sneak through the border in the middle of the night. He had his plan chalked out. Once inside India, he would look for the thickest part of the forest and climb up one of the tall conifers. There he would sit and wait for a patrol to pass by. That would be his target.

Just like any other morning, Major Deepak Arora was leading the patrol, all charged up and eager for an encounter. About five feet behind him was his JCO Tej Bahadur Thapa scanning each and every corner with his X-ray vision. Behind him with a gap of about six feet between them, ten other Gorkhas followed. They were taking a turn around a crevasse so that they had made a complete semicircle.

Sher Khan had initially planned to fire from his position at the top of the tree. But when he saw the Major right under his tree about ten feet away with all the other Gorkhas in the form of a sickle, he changed his plan. He wanted to kill all of them at one go and he wanted to do it in style. After all it would be his signature kill.

As Deepak was carefully scanning the other end of the crevasse, a huge Pathan with his face covered in black cloth, dropped from the tree right in front of him, fingers on the trigger of his AK-47, ready to fire.

Sher Khan's plan was to take the Major first and then the rest at one go before anyone could react. He was sure the surprise element would work in his favor. Surprised and shocked he was as, his most trusted friend for years, who had been with him through thick and thin, betrayed him. The AK-47 was jammed and would not fire. He could not believe his luck as he looked up at the Major standing not even five feet away from him.

Deepak was petrified. His legs were frozen and senses gone numb, he stood there like a statue holding his carbine pointed towards his enemy.

'Patak-Dhoom.'

The sound of a fire and the bullet wheezing past his ears brought him back to his senses as he saw the tall Pathan lying on the ground, with a clean shot through the head. His JCO was quick to react.

"*Hazur, thikchha*?" Tej Bahadur was concerned.

"Yea, I am fine." whispered an enthralled Deepak with a deflated ego, "Let's head back to the post."

Deepak was sitting in his living bunker, all alone. The sense of fear was leaving him as acute embarrassment took over. He knew weapons too well to realize that the probability of an AK-47 not firing was one in a billion. He knew how lucky he had been. As he sat on the corner of his bed holding his head down, the bullet hanging around his neck popped out. He held it in his hand, smiled and picked up the phone to connect to the operator.

"Connect me to my wife."

"Puja?" was all he could say as she picked up the phone.

"Deepak, are you fine? You sound terrible!"

"I have never felt any better dear. When is your passport expiring?"

"Not in the recent future I presume. But why?" shouted Puja.

"I am coming down to Delhi tomorrow. We are going for a tour of Europe."

Puja was mesmerized.

Parsimonious Uncle Scrooge never wanted to let go of his second chance.

✦ ✦ ✦

4

Plebeian

A commoner (as used in ancient Roman) was the definition that stared back at Horigopal Ghosh from the yellow and torn pages of the Oxford dictionary as he tried to find the meaning of the word Plebeian. It was just yesterday when someone in his office referred to him by this word and he had no other option but to pass a sheepish smile back, not having understood what it meant. All he understood at that point in time was that his young and successful office colleague had more of ridicule and sarcasm in his tone than respect. Now, back in his small attic room near Beleghata, North Kolkata, surrounded by his old books and clothes he couldn't help but smile once again. *A plebeian I was, a plebeian I am and a plebeian is what I will be till my last day...*

Horigopal Ghosh, commonly known as Hori, typically represented the millions of the office going population on the ever busy streets of Kolkata. People who would swarm the streets of Kolkata during the morning and evening hours trying to put their best foot forward to reach office on time (if only they would get a place to put their foot). You would find them either compressed like elastic balls deep down in a bus, hanging like bats from the door handles and windows of the trams or pushing themselves inside the metro even as the door would refuse to close. Hori was just another face. One more number in that uncountable population still trying to prove Darwin's theory of evolutionary survival of the fittest.

In his mid-forties, standing at not more than five feet six inches, slightly potbellied and bald, wearing a thin moustache and a tortoise shell spectacle, when Hori would walk on the streets of Kolkata with his office bag and his lunch box tucked under the arm, no one would bother to pass him a second glance. He remembered a friend of his having told him once: "Hori, you know you are a perfect fit in the espionage world. RAW actually picks up people like you so that they don't stand out in the crowd. If you pass through a place or you meet someone it is very difficult to recall your features as you are never conspicuous!"

This was many years back, but he had never forgotten his friend's word. So much as to secretly nurture this dream of being picked up by RAW one day. As at the end of each grueling day after having his dinner at Joga's small roadside shop and walking up to his empty attic room, he had the reverie of becoming a man of significance one day. Not that his current status bothered him a lot. He had accepted his destiny and himself just like a mother accepts her differently able child. But that evening after having discovered the true meaning of the word Plebeian he realized the derogatory undertone that was hidden in the comment made in office. What hurt him more was that everyone around in office also expressed their tacit acceptance of the truth. In our lives we all have our share of harsh truths that we carry with us, truths about our own selves which we tuck away in the deepest corner of our mind to lead a compromised co-existence. However, if those are discovered by someone else and certified, the peaceful co-existence disrupts and the dormant demon creates turmoil within us. This is what happened to Hori. All of a sudden he could no longer accept himself and felt gloomy. He couldn't sleep well that night. A loner by nature his sole friend in his room was a fat gecko. Even that seemed to be echoing the thought in its tik-tik-tik monotone.

The next day, as Hori reached office, he looked quite tired. Dasbabu, the only person in the office with whom Hori ever spoke observed his crestfallen look and approached his desk, "Horibabu, what's wrong? You look ill! Did you sleep well last night?"

"Honestly no, Dasbabu. I couldn't. Something was bothering me all night," replied a tired Hori.

"Hmm...you know what? I think you should be taking few days off. When was the last time you ever took a holiday?"

To this Hori pondered a while and replied, "I don't even remember. I think it must have been five years back when my Mom expired."

"See? The work is getting on you. Listen to me. Take a few days off and relax. You are a religious man. Why don't you go to Maha Kumbh Mela? If I am not wrong, it's sometime this month at Allahabad. I am sure you will like it."

Somehow this idea struck a chord in Hori's disturbed mind and he decided to go on this holy trip. He had always wanted to go to the Maha Kumbh Mela, but somehow that never clicked.

Getting leave approved from the boss was a cake walk as he hardly ever applied for one. Thus Hori finally felt light hearted as he left office that day. There were still almost ten days left for the holy ablution, but he decided to leave early for Allahabad and spend some time enjoying the surroundings.

As Hori got down at the Allahabad station early in the morning, he realized the suffocating office crowd of Kolkata was just a stream compared to this ocean of people. There were millions of people belonging to all castes, creeds, social status, countries and religions who had gathered there to take a holy dip in that auspicious hour. This Maha Kumbh was their only chance to attain moksha. It's was now or never, because only once in 144 years would they get to see this unique combination of spiritual energies. According to astrologers, the Kumbh Mela took place when the planet Jupiter entered the sign of Aquarius and the Sun entered into Aries. But to Hori what was closest to his heart was the mythical story told to him by his Ma, so many times in his childhood. He still remembered how he would listen to her with bated breath and undivided attention as she would take him to the world of Gods and demons. The demons or asuras were relentlessly fighting with their peace-loving brothers, the Gods or *devatas*. One day, the gods went to Vishnu and asked for help. Vishnu asked them to churn the milky ocean which would give them a pot of golden nectar, an elixir to immortality. As soon as the golden pot came out from the churn, Dhanwantari, the primordial physician, leapt forward, grabbed the pot of nectar and ran away. The demons, quicker than him, pursued him relentlessly. This long chase lasted 12 days, which were equivalent to 12 years on earth. During this chase, which traversed all realms of the universe, Dhanwantari rested only four times, placing the Kumbh on the ground as each time few drops of the holy nectar spilled out. These four places – Nasik, Ujjain, Hardwar and Allahabad – are today the centers of the Kumbh Mela.

The god fearing Hori, never doubted the authenticity of the mythical stories and firmly believed that this was his only chance to absolve in the holy nectar. He was in an infinite melting pot and wanted to just flow in the immense tide. He decided to put up in one of the multiple tents set up by the authorities. It had a very basic arrangement but to his relief was reasonably clean. He wanted to be as near to the confluence as possible and this tent gave him that opportunity to view the expanse of the Ganges. It was January and the cold wind gave him shivers as he tried to breathe in the wet air. He looked all around to realize that this was a confluence of the whole of India and beyond. Millions of people with their trillion dreams had all adjusted and accommodated themselves in that area for a common goal. No one fought with anyone; everyone was ready to help the person next to him. As he stood there mystified by the atmosphere his eyes got moist and he wished his mom were there. Who could have guessed the drama to unfold in the days to come!

Early next morning, before sunrise Hori decided to use the common toilets next to the tents. He knew that the early bird would get the prize of a cleaner washroom. However since he had never ever used a common toilet ever in his life, he had no clue of the logistic challenges. He was wearing his usual shirt and trousers with a pullover on top and found it extremely difficult to undress outside and get in the toilet due to the chill. The inside of the toilet was also very small to manage things. As he was standing there pondering what to do a Sadhu happened to observe his dilemma. He smiled and approached Hori and softly said, "Beta, it seems this is your first time in this kind of a religious gathering?"

"Yes, Sir," replied Hori reverently. "But how could you make it out?"

To this the saintly old man just smiled and handed over a red robe to him and said, "Wear this piece of cloth. This will help you till you are here. Western dresses are not very convenient in pilgrimage. Also, I see you are carrying lot of weight inside you. It's time you shed that and get into something new."

Hori was deeply touched by the action of this stranger. As he looked up from examining the robe, he realized that the sadhu was gone. He had vanished in some nano seconds.

Who was he? Where had he come from and how could he have evaporated like that? How did he even know that I was sad from inside?

So many questions he had that dawn, but all he could hear was the echo of his own thoughts coming back from the bank of the Ganges. He sighed, looked at the impressive piece of red cloth and decided to put it on. To his surprise he realized the convenience of wearing it in a place like this. Happy, he returned to his tent, kept back his own clothes and decided to go for a stroll near the banks.

The preparation for the most auspicious day was under full swing. The main barricades and security were already in place. He could see the different *Akhras* for the sadhus. He was surprised to see that even amongst them who had apparently given up all materialistic belongings to enter this phase in their lives, there was a caste system. They had their own categorization and priority to the time of the holy dip! It was as if they had renounced life to get into yet another complex one. What was the purpose then? While Hori was walking, lost in his thought, something strange had happened. Something that Hori was too preoccupied to observe. All the people around were giving him way with reverence and had started paying respect to him by saying namaste. Initially he thought they were meant for someone else and ignored. However, when an elderly lady all of a sudden threw herself at his feet shouting, "Baba, please save me," Hori was petrified. He still had not realized what had happened. As he looked around he saw a crowd gathering to observe the drama as the old lady lay on the floor, dead as a log not letting go of his legs. Used to being taken for granted, Hori couldn't fathom why he had been thrown into the limelight all of a sudden.

The robe...people have mistaken me for a sadhu!!!

Embarrassed to the core, he lifted the lady up and said, "Ma, please, forgive me. I am not the one you think..."

"Baba, you are the one. I have seen it in your eyes. Only you can help me. Please don't send me away," cried the lady.

As Hori looked into the sad, sunken and desolate eyes of the lady something stopped him from forcing her away. This lonely lady in tattered clothes roaming from pilgrimage to pilgrimage seeking eternal solace could have been his mom.

"What is bothering you Ma?" he asked politely holding her hand.

"My son, Baba, whom I gave my entire life to foster, whom I got educated, working all day and night as a widow, threw me out of the house after getting married. I am yet to come out of the shock Baba and go around all pilgrimages to seek some peace." Beyond this she could say no more as she stood there holding Hori's hand.

Hori was overwhelmed. His eyes got moist as he gently whispered to her, "Ma, you are looking for peace at all wrong places. A mother can find peace only with her children. Have you tried going back to him? Maybe he is repenting and desperately wants to have you back but has no clue where to find you! Listen to me, go back and meet him."

Hori could immediately see the flicker of hope coming back in those distant eyes as she thanked him and walked away.

Overawed and speechless Hori slowly walked back to his tent and sat down on the bed. The tent was empty as he held his head in the cusp of his hands and contemplated for a while.

What is happening to me? A nonentity on the streets of Kolkata, I, Horigopal Ghosh, have been esteemed as a saint? Is it the charisma of this place, the blindfolded faith of the people or some magical power of this red robe? I don't know. But this whole thing is pricking me from within. All my life I have led a simple and honest life. But now I feel I am cheating on these people by taking undue advantage of their faith. These people are all prisoners of their own sufferings and deeds. All I am doing is making them play to their own tune.

Disgusted with himself, he got up to take off the robe. But just as he was about to, someone from deep within whispered in his ear, "Come on Hori. This is what you had always dreamt of, to be a man of significance one day. Here you have that opportunity. It's just matter of few days. No one knows you here, just go ahead and live your dream."

Hori couldn't stop himself from being enticed.

What followed in the days to come was phenomenal. That old lady must have passed her word around as from the next day onwards more people started coming to him. As he walked on the streets he could feel prying eyes looking at him. He could overhear their soft gossip as they referred to him as Bangali Baba. The tent authority person also came down to him to ensure arrangements were to his satisfaction. Hori was basking in his new found publicity. However, deep within, he was never dishonest to the people who walked up to him for help. He soon realized that this world was full of human prototypes carrying their unsatisfied souls with them seeking instant remedy that never existed. But what he did was give sincere attention and listen to their pain as if it were his own. He would let them empty their heavy vessel, something that they might have been carrying for decades. Then finally when they felt lighter having shed their grief he would give them very simple, down to earth and basic advice. That would do the trick, as it is always the pathetically mundane and simple counseling that struck a chord in people's minds. Hori was gleefully accepted by the masses as one of their own, yet, above them. Thus went the days and nights. Thus grew Bangali Baba's fame and thus, people came to him in grief and went back elated.

The final day arrived with the auspicious hour for the holy ablution starting at five in the morning and lasting for a few hours only. Everyone wanted to take a dip during that time and hence the security was all geared up and prepared to handle the enormous rush. Thirteen sects of sadhus lead bathers in a mutually agreed-on sequence.

The fraternity was led by Maha Nirvani Akhada and was followed by Niranjani, Anand, Juna and Bairagiakahadas, among others.

As the clock struck five, heavily decked-up chariots, some in silver and gold, wound their way to the Sangam, with hundreds following in procession on foot, beating drums and blowing conch shells. Carrying silver tridents, maces, axes and swords, some of the sadhus with flowing beards shouted, "*Ganga Mayiya ki jay!*" as they rushed towards the water. Several rows of sand bags had been piled up on the three-kilometer bathing stretch and deep water barricading had been done up to avoid mishaps.

Hori was transfixed. Even in his new avatar, he had no clue how to reach the water and cleanse himself. But his status helped him again. His devotees ensured that he entered the holy water without much hassle.

And there he was, standing waist deep in the chilly nectar kissed water, all by himself. He could almost hear his Ma narrating the story next to his ears as the electrifying atmosphere sent shivers through his spine. He felt as if he was standing on the same place where Dhanwantari had rested when the demons chased him. Detaching himself from all thoughts, Hori took a deep breath and dipped inside the Ganges. He would not remember for how long he was inside that icy droning cocoon, but when he got up he felt an inner peace he had never felt before. He felt one with the entire Universe.

After ten odd minutes he came out of the water and slowly started walking back to his tent. His purpose was fulfilled. He felt very calm from within. As he reached his tent he realized people had not yet returned from their baths and the entire area was empty. He dried himself, took off his robe and changed into his trouser and shirt. Very slowly he packed his carry bag, came out of the tent to very delicately hang the wet robe on the wire and slowly walked towards the crowd. As the red spectral arms of the robe fluttered in the air trying desperately to beckon him back, he just turned back and smiled.

Once more he was just another face in the crowd. He had already started missing his old, dilapidated attic room. He craved to see the face of his gecko friend on the wall. He felt severe hunger pangs for Joga's mutton curry and rice.

A plebeian I was, a plebeian I am and a plebeian is what I would always like to be...

✦ ✦ ✦

5

Hunger

As the rebellious cry touched the blue firmament, announcing the arrival of a whitish little being, Pushpita's first son, Karan was born. Pushpita too cried that night, but those were the tears of joy as she touched her newborn hope with her frail hands.

It was never easy to have seen this day. It took her and Poritosh ten grueling years with multiple visits to doctors, quacks, gurus and temples to have a child of their own. Finally modern science made that possible. Who was born that night was not just their child but beyond. Karan was a bundle of crystallized hope, a reflection of the past and a seed for their dreams.

As the nurse moved the newborn to the cabin after few hours, Pushpita looked at her son with moist eyes and felt an immediate and overwhelming sense of motherhood overpowering her. She then gently placed Karan next to her breasts to help him suckle, but he rejected. Pushpita thought that maybe she had not yet started lactating and should wait for a while. Tired and exhausted she put her reassuring hand on Karan and surrendered to Morpheus. She couldn't recall how much time had gone by as she suddenly woke up to Karan's loud cry. Assuming he was hungry, she again tried feeding him. To her surprise he vehemently rejected this time too! This worried Pushpita as she called the nurse who came running to the alarm bell.

"Sister, something is wrong. He looks hungry, but is rejecting my milk!"

"Don't worry Didi. Sometimes the milk comes a bit late. You relax, I will feed him Lactogen. He should be fine."

With this the Nurse picked up Karan and walked out of the room. The frantic sound gradually faded behind the closed door unlike the myriad folds on Pushpita's forehead. She laid back and pondered about what could be wrong?

As Poritosh walked in the room after a while, she looked even more worried and was restless.

"Pori, please go and check whether Karan is fine. He was crying like anything a little while back. He wouldn't even accept my milk!"

"Now now, Pushp, don't get so worked up. These things happen with small babies. It's natural. These people are experts. Let them handle him."

After having consoled his wife, Poritosh walked out of the room towards the nursery to enquire. The nurses were all busy either bathing or feeding the many bundles of joy. Finally the nurse, who was taking care of Pushpita, walked up to him with a smile.

"Sir, your son is fine and is sleeping. Do you see him at the remote corner? That's him."

Yes, Karan was sleeping peacefully like an Angel as if he had not yet detached himself from the world he had come from.

"But why was he crying Sister?"

"Oh, that? Normal with babies...that's their natural response. How else do you think they can grab our attention?" She smile.

"Hmm...but did he drink some milk?"

"Well...honestly, he didn't. He rejected the milk as I tried to feed him. However, as I rocked him a bit he fell asleep. So there is nothing to worry. Sometimes babies start feeding only after a while."

A hardcore accountant by profession and having always run miles away from biology books, Poritosh had no other option but to believe whatever the sister conveyed to him.

Natural response is it? How unnatural it sounds when it pierces your brain! Can't they have some better way of drawing attention? Like ringing a bell or just waving a hand and politely saying 'Hi!'

With all these thoughts looming over his head, he went back to the room to find Pushpita deep asleep.

The soft melody of the Magpie Robin woke Poritosh up quite early in the morning. He got up from the bed to realize that Pushpita was not in the room. Alarmed, he jumped out of the bed and after having checked the washroom went out in the main lobby. He could hear his wife's animated conversation with the nurses from a distance. A group of two-three nurses had gathered in front of the nursery and were trying to convince Pushpita of something. Seeing Poritosh, she came running to him. Panting she said, "Pori, there is something wrong and these Sisters are trying to hide it from me. Karan has not drunk a single drop of milk the entire night. Every time they would try to feed him he would react the same way and throw out the milk! How is that possible? Please call Dr. Malhotra immediately. Let him check."

Poritosh had also started to fret. However, he didn't let that come on his face and said, "Don't get so upset Pushpi. Let me talk to the Sisters."

"Sister, is there something to worry? Has Dr. Malhotra been notified?"

"Sir, usually by now the babies start accepting milk, be it their own mom's or from outside. This is a bit unusual, but maybe Didi can try feeding him once more. Doctor is on his way and should be in shortly."

Pushpita also was a bit pacified by this explanation and went back to her room with Karan. As she tried to feed him, it was the same reaction that followed. An outright rejection ornamented with a loud protest.

As Dr. Vineet Malhotra, a handsome young man in his mid-thirties, entered the room about fifteen minutes later, the atmosphere had become as gloomy as a monsoon sky. Pushpita sat at the corner of the bed holding her forehead as Poritosh tried to console her. Karan, however was peacefully asleep in his cot blissfully unaware of the happenings of this mundane world. The Sisters had already updated the doctor on his way as he straight away went to the sleeping child and started examining him.

"Is he sleeping well? Is he being cranky all the time? What's his weight?" Dr. Malhotra bombarded the sister with multiple questions to assess the situation. After all his queries were answered he sat down in the sofa and started to ponder.

"Hmmm...interesting. You see Mr. Dutta," he said addressing Poritosh, "Your son has not taken any nutrient from outside since he was born. It's been more than twenty four hours now. But the interesting part is that he is behaving absolutely normal. Just like any other child on his or her second day! His heartbeat is normal, his chest is clear, he is not cranky and having a regular sleeping pattern!"

"Then why is he not drinking any milk Doctor?" shouted Pushpita in trepidation.

"Honestly, Ma'am, we don't have an answer now. We will put him under observation where all his body functions would be closely monitored for the next forty eight hours. Be patient. You should be happy that he is behaving normally."

With this Dr. Malhotra left the room after instructing the Sister to transfer Karan to the monitoring room. As Karan was taken away his parents sat quietly on the bed holding each other's hand soaked in heavy silence. Pushpita couldn't hold herself anymore and started to sob uncontrollably. As the tear drops traveled down and touched her husband's hand, he thought 'What have we done to deserve this? Ten years of prayers, a decade of delicately nurtured dreams...all to see this day? We never wanted a boy or a girl in particular! All we ever wished for was someone special with the most ordinary behavior and intelligence to come and fill in our empty space. Oh Lord...why us?'

The next few days went by shrouded with anxiety, fear, monitoring and consultation as Karan consistently refused to suckle. What surprised the medical world the most was that notwithstanding him not having taken any food since he was born four days back, he not only exhibited normal pattern but also gained weight!!! How was that possible? The entire medical world was flabbergasted and started studying the baby as if he was a medical case, a model beyond any human feelings.

What they were not ready to accept was Karan's birth beyond Science. He was born beyond human logic. He was beyond our world that we perceive, the principles we believe. He belonged to an alien microcosm where the most basic human need was an uncalled for noise, a disturbance in the serene lake. Karan had defied Hunger!

Five years went by since that miraculous day. Pushpita and Poritosh took some time to overcome their grief and accept Karan as he was. What was more important to them was Karan behaved just like any other child. The medical world was stunned and the media had got a meaty story to chase as things started getting out of control. Karan was being dragged around to his parents dislike. So they decided to move out of the town and settle in a not so well known place, to start life afresh. Poritosh was reluctant but with Pushpita's relentless pestering he finally gave in. He realized that may be it would be the best thing for Karan. In a new place if dealt tactfully no one would ever get to know this secret and he would be accepted as a normal child.

And so they started their unknown journey in an even more unknown place surrounded with new faces. Poritosh took up a clerical job in a small office as Pushpita started raising their child with all her love and angst. As the years went by, Karan kept growing every day both in health and mind. He was like an orchid growing on top of a big oak, getting its entire nutrient from the air. His parents like the oak sheltered him from this cruel and chary world with their myriad branches and thick foliage.

Day in and day out Karan nurtured this secret inside him. His parents had strictly instructed him never to share this with anyone ever. He was told to accept this as part of him and behave normally. But how easy was it? Did anyone try to touch and feel his heavy heart when during the school recess all his friends eagerly checked out each other's tiffin box to share the food? Could anyone ever understand the grief that embraced him when he saw the celestial pleasure on the face of a child greedily finishing an ice cream on a hot summer afternoon? The entire world to him was full of aliens as he tried to breathe their air and cope up.

With all these complex thoughts intertwined, Karan stepped into his teens. He had grown into an extremely intelligent individual and would excel in all quarters of Life. However, with maturity he realized he didn't have the answers to so many things. His unique character made him look at this world with a completely different perspective. Every individual was struggling to survive. They all had to earn to eat and eat to live. As his neighbor ran to catch the office bus with a disgusted look, as their maid ran from one house to the other carrying her eight month daughter along, as his school and college friends fervently argued over a suitable career, as siblings withdrew from each other fighting over ancestral property, as sons threw their parents on the street, as children grew hungry in the streets of Somalia, as religious flame of frenzy scorched thousands of innocent souls...he would sit back and think how much of it would have made sense in his world?

Thus he thought and thus he grew, strung between these two disparate worlds of greed and solace, anguish and ecstasy, dystopia and utopia. He could never make up his mind where he wanted to be and what would make him happy, till Deepika walked into his life.

Deepika, an ever chirpy girl moved next door along with her parents during a sultry summer afternoon. Tall, dusky and extremely lean it was difficult to comprehend from where she got her infinite exuberance. She was such a compulsive communicator that when everyone around her would retire to her endless drone she would start talking to the mirror! Her large innocent eyes could have melted the darkest of the souls.

Karan saw her for the first time as he was relaxing on his terrace in a breezy evening.

"Hey you!" shouted Deepika from the adjacent terrace trying to draw Karan's attention.

Karan, oblivious of her presence and lost deep within his own world, could hardly hear.

"Hey, Mr. Whatever, I am talking to you. Can you hear me?"

To this Karan leaned his head to find this girl shouting and jumping on the adjacent terrace trying to draw his attention.

"Yes, how can I help you?" Karan said indifferently.

"You can start by letting me know your name, then pick the ripe guava from the tree overhanging your terrace and throw it over!"

"Guava? Which one?" Karan searched as he had never ever felt the desire to look for one!

"The one right there." She pointed.

Karan smiled as he got up picked up the fruit and threw it over to her." There you go and my name is Karan."

Deepika smiled back and said, "This is Deepika, thanks."

Thus through a frivolous conversation was born that day a relationship to last a lifetime. Deepika happened to study in the same college as Karan. For some unexplainable reason they started liking each other as friends. What Karan liked in her was her carefree attitude towards life and accepting each moment as is. She would never be inquisitive about Karan's past and ask him any questions. Every time she would eat something and offer him the same Karan would mildly refuse. But she would never ever probe beyond that. She had just asked him once, "Don't you feel hungry?" To that he had replied, "I don't eat outside my house."

Beyond that she never ever broached this topic. But Karan knew that it was just matter of time that she would find out.

Deepika had her own reasons to like Karan. She found this intelligent, handsome and philanthropic person always pregnant with an ocean deep thought, a thought he had befriended but still not accepted.

Time flowed like crystal clear water in the brook making their bond stronger every moment. It would have flowed like this forever, had that evening not arrived....

It had got late that day in college due to an extra class. Karan and Deepika just like every day started walking back home, chatting on the way. It was winter and had got dark early. The road that they generally would take was completely deserted. As they were approaching the church area, they could see a group of ruffians sitting across the street playing cards. They were abusing and shouting at the top of their voices and creating a nuisance. Deepika got scared and held Karan's arm, "Let's take another route Karan," she said pensively. "Relax Deepika, just stay close to me, nothing will happen," said Karan calmly. With this he started walking along the road ensuring Deepika was close to him. As they approached the group, one of them passed an obscene remark towards Deepika and tried to hold her hand. Getting a lead, the other three also got up and tried getting close to her. An attractive girl in a deserted street accompanied by a young lad pushed their desire to an extreme. What none of them including Deepika knew was that Karan was a karate black belt and religiously practiced his skills every morning. Before Deepika could blink an eye all four were lying on the floor writhing in acute pain and bleeding from their noses. Karan stood there calm as a cucumber observing them with utter disgust. As he looked at their distorted faces hiding an even distorted mind, he thought that these characters would have existed in his world too.

Deepika was flustered to the core. She hid herself in Karan's chest and couldn't move. Karan gently pulled her away from the scene and started walking away. None of them spoke a word that evening. They just slowly walked towards their home hand in hand looking much ahead of what their pair of eyes could see. They felt that a moment had slipped through time to bring them so close. The chilly winter breeze was sarcastically defied by the warmth of the two bodies that evening. As they were about to reach their homes, Deepika slowly withdrew her hand and gently kissed Karan on the cheek. Then she ran inside her house. She had a strange feeling all over her body. She realized she was in love. That night as her Mom asked her to join them for dinner she refused.

"I am not hungry Ma...you carry on."

Karan slowly walked inside his house and went straight to his room and lay down on his bed, still wrapped up in her sweet touch. He was also having a strange feeling all over his body. He realized he was in love. But beyond the warm glow he felt a strange rumbling in his stomach. It was an acute cramping pain which was unbearable, a pain which he had never ever experienced in his life. After eighteen dry years of herculean fasting, Karan was finally overwhelmed by an insatiable hunger for food!

Love, the universal remedy to all maladies had bridged the apparently infinite gap between Karan's two disparate worlds.

✦ ✦ ✦

6

Village Specter

Teenage is a very interesting stage in life. We stand at the crossroads of life with half-baked intellect, beliefs, principles and anatomy trying to argue and defy all treaded paths. The two most favorite and widely discussed topics are the existence of God and Ghost. Born out of the human mind and beliefs, based hardly on any first hand evidence, these two age-old dogmas are mercilessly attacked by the teenagers treating them as bias of the Homo sapiens' evolved brains.

Today as I look back over my shoulders a few decades, I realize to my amusement, I was no exception. Desperately trying to grow that thin line on top of my lips and fashioning an imposter baritone to hide the embarrassing croaky voice, I was, to say the least, insensitive to the world. I had just celebrated my sixteenth birthday as I announced myself to this world as an atheist. Disrespecting the age, belief or sentiment of anyone, I would surgically cut through using sound logic and vanquish the existence of God. The concept of ghost to me was even more ludicrous as I was sanguine it was nothing but a figment of imagination and fear.

"Why don't we see ghosts during the day?" used to be my trump card question during the marathon debates. I would justify human mind being afraid of the dark to create these shadowy images.

"Why don't you think animals see ghosts?" I would challenge them as I would explain what we see is what we imagine.

So I was gallantly trotting on my shinning black horse of overconfidence and pride like a Knight, ruthlessly decapitating any challenger on my way, when I stumbled upon something quite unexpected.

It was the month of October. My school had closed for the Durga Puja. I had a month long vacation that only the students of West Bengal still have the privilege to enjoy during the month of this festival....

According to Hindu mythology it is believed that every year, Goddess Durga mounted on a lion visits the Earth for four days along with her daughters Saraswati and Lakshmi and sons Ganesha and Kartikeya. Some also believe that every year she changes her mode of transportation. She has four other modes of transportation besides the Lion, each mode signifying something. An elephant denotes prosperity and good harvest while a palanquin is an indication of natural calamities. The horse signifies drought and a boat indicates heavy rain and floods.

To all our dismay, that year she decided to arrive on a boat. Dark cloud and heavy rain since the auspicious day of *Mahalaya* dampened the festive spirit all around. Everyone held onto the thin ray of hope that the rain would pass away and sunshine would bless them during the Puja. I never had much hope and neither did the weather department, which back during those days was quite unreliable. I was a typical Kolkata fanatic who come what may, would never ever move out of the City of Joy during the Durga Puja. But surprisingly, this time I was feeling a bit bored and wanted to take this opportunity to move away from the hub nub for a few days.

My dad's elder sister was a widow and lived all alone in a remote village in West Bengal, about two hours of train journey away from Kolkata. I had been there a number of times and each time smitten by the virgin beauty of that land I had felt like staying back forever. Urban development was yet to reach the interiors of rural Bengal, especially where my aunt stayed. My mind made up, I decided to give her a surprise.

"Oh My God, Bapi! What a pleasant surprise and that too during the Puja? Come in, come in," *Pishi* (as father's sister is referred to in Bengali) was elated seeing me.

"Don't get so worked up Pishi, I am not running away till the Puja ends. So relax. Come here and sit next to me. How are you?" I tried to get her excited state tone down to normalcy as she had started jumping here and there not knowing what she should do to make me comfortable.

"Where is Dada? He was supposed to come during the Puja right?" I inquired.

"Your Dada has very much come. He has gone to pick something from the corner shop, should be here any time. He will be ecstatic seeing you. This very morning, he was talking about you. You go to your favorite room Bapi and freshen up. I will get something for you to eat. You must be tired."

My Dada or cousin brother was Pishi's only son. He was a Chemical Engineer and worked in Mumbai. But every year during the Puja he ensured that he came and spent some time with her. He was just like a real brother to me and in spite of him being twelve years elder we interacted more as friends.

The cycle bell followed by heavy footsteps up the stairs told me Dada had come and already knew of my presence.

"This is telepathy Bapi, can't be anything else. I was talking about you today only." He shouted as he gave me a bear hug.

"I know Dada, Pishi was telling me," I smiled back.

"You don't know how relieved I am seeing you. I landed up yesterday and was already feeling bored. You know Bapi, it's just Ma for whom I make this trip each year. I have asked her so many times to come and stay with me. But she is adamant and would never leave this house. I don't understand what is left in this dilapidated mansion," Dada was irritated.

"It's not about the house Dada, it's the memories associated with it, you know that and we have discussed this at length in the past. Anyway, let's not get into that. Now that I am here, let's make the best of the few days we are together."

Overloaded with a sumptuous lunch and ruminating a sweet betel leaf or *misti* paan, Dada and I decided to laze on the coir mattress on the roof. This house had always fascinated me. Decrepit and damaged beyond repair in most of the areas, these bricks stood as a testimony of time.

"What are you thinking?" Dada asked me, as I had not spoken a word since we had come to the roof top.

"Nothing," I replied.

"Bapi, don't lie. I can sense something is going on in your mind. Now come clean."

"Dada, can we do it this time?" I looked at him with pleading eyes.

"You have still not grown out of that old fascination of yours? How many times do I need to tell you it's not worth it."

"Dada please, every time you refuse. This time I am not going to listen. If you don't come along, I will go all alone tonight. If something befalls me you would be responsible," I blackmailed him.

"God, why are you doing this to me? What if Ma gets to know?" I had seen the thin ray of hope...he was considering!

"We will not tell her Dada. We will go late in the night after she has slept off and would be back before dawn." I assured.

"You have put me in an odd position, but okay, I will do it for you. Remember this is the first and the last time," he clarified strongly.

I jumped up and hugged him. I was so happy. Finally it would be a dream come true for me.

"Okay, okay, don't overdo it. Listen, I have some friend to meet in the evening. I will walk down. You take my cycle and move around. We will meet at dusk."

My Pishi's village, as I have already mentioned was quite backward in those days. You would be surprised to know that the village didn't even have the basic privilege of electricity. For me it was like a journey in the time machine. It fascinated and pulled me back each time. There was yet another attraction, which, unfulfilled for long, had by then not only grown bigger but become an obsession.

The village burning ghat...

Now don't jump to imagining today's state of the art burning ghats with electric incinerators. I am talking of decades back and that too in a remote village in Bengal. No electricity meant the absence of any incinerators. People still used the time tested method of burning the dead using firewood.

The village burning ghat was situated at the farthest corner to the west next to a small river locally known as Kopila. If not told, a stranger could never make out that it was a burning ghat. Completely barren with the jackals as frequent visitors, the only identifying landmark was the dead banyan tree. Struck with high voltage lightning, who knows when, it stood right in the middle of the burning ghat as the sole companion of the dead. Black, naked, morbid and desolate it stood there with its thousand arms stretched out towards the sky praying for freedom from its eternal embarrassment.

I don't know whether it was the tree or the place which attracted me like a magnet every time. Whatever it was, it was not to be quenched by my daytime rendezvous. My desire was to spend a night there, right in the middle of the burning ghat, hand in hand with the dead, putting my faith of non-existence of ghosts and afterlife to the ultimate acid test. It was this obsession of mine that my Dada was vehemently trying to reject and which to my ecstasy I won.

I had been waywardly cycling for a while, burning my energy and enjoying nature, when I realized I had come quite far away from Pishi's house. The unpolluted western sky had been painted fluorescent orange as the birds were chirruping to return to the safety of their nests. Tired, I stopped, still on the cycle with my legs on the ground, to enjoy the ethereal bliss. Suddenly it dawned on me that I had inadvertently reached the burning ghat as I could see the hapless banyan tree to my left about hundred yards away. Lonely and rejected as ever, its myriad arms seemed to be beckoning me in the dwindling light. I stood there mesmerized.

A faint movement on the lowest branch of the tree caught my attention. It seemed to be a white piece of cloth. As I tried to gaze to make out what it was, my legs got numb. What was hanging from the branch was not just a piece of cloth but a man, wearing a dhoti with a rope around his neck, lifeless yet swaying in the wind. Had it been a comfortable drawing room back in Kolkata, I am sure I would have laughed at the situation and proved my virtual bravery. But that evening, standing all alone in that vanishing twilight, I realized that quickly cycling back to the shelter of my Pishi's house was the wisest decision.

"What is wrong Bapi? You look awful!" shouted Dada as I entered the house.

I sat down on the chair and after regaining my composure gave him a detailed description of what I had seen.

"Hmm. You see Bapi, committing suicide by either drinking pesticide or hanging by the neck is pretty common in villages. But this being a small village such news spreads like fire. However, I have not heard of this from any one this evening. Maybe it happened very late, just before you went there. Generally, people don't venture near the ghat late in the evenings and hence no one knows. Tomorrow morning the news might spread. Anyway, it's good in one way. Tonight's program stands canceled," uttered my relieved Dada.

Deep within, I was also hesitant about the plan. Today, sitting and pondering about the past, I have no shame to confess that I was afraid. It was my very first encounter with death. I was shaken from inside. But you should remember that back then I was harnessing a pride and an inflated ego, something I could not let go at any cost.

"I will go," I whispered.

"What? Have you lost your mind Bapi? Do you even know what you are saying? There is this dead body hanging there and you want to go there and spend a night with it?" Dada was furious.

"Dada, it's just a dead body, a cask which has been made devoid of life, as good or bad as the lifeless tree. What is there to be afraid of? Come to think of it Dada, this would be a golden chance to test the existence of ghosts. If today we can spend the night there and come back unscathed, we would prove for certain it's all in our mind."

"Whom do you want to prove and for what? How does it even matter whether they exist or not? Let them be and you also be happy."

"No Dada, I can't let a chance like this go fruitlessly. I will go, whether you want to come or not it is your wish," I was adamant.

"Bapi, you are crossing your limit. I will inform Ma about it now," he warned.

"Okay, go ahead, but remember this would be my last visit to your place then," I was again using my blackmailing technique, it always worked with him.

"You are again pushing me. Okay, we will go, but if I see the body still there, we will immediately come back. Deal?"

"Deal, deal and a deal," I shouted as I again hugged him.

When we were tiptoeing out of the house to ensure Pishi would not wake up, it was exactly midnight. The somber toll of the grandfather clock, the soft hoot of the Barn owl and the call of the Nightjar all tried to warn us, as we stepped on the mud road equipped with our courage and a pair of five cell torches. We decided to walk down as cycling in the night would have been even bigger a challenge. An unhurried walk through the rice fields would take us close to an hour.

Living in the city, I had completely forgotten how beautiful night could be. The sky was dazzling with myriad stars. It was as if the day sky had been covered with a black sheet with million holes in it. The moon was so strong that we could almost see our own shadows. None of us spoke. We never wanted to break the rhythm of silence we were encompassed in, in that cosmic hour. By the time we reached our destination it was close to one. The unvanquished banyan stood there, even darker. But as both of us tried to scan its branches, we were surprised. There was no dead man hanging from any of the branches.

"Bapi, are you sure you saw what you saw?" Dada was obviously incredulous.

"Dada, come on. How can I make such a visual error?"

"Hmm, then the relatives must have come and taken it away."

"Maybe...," I mumbled.

"Let's walk across the ghat and go near the river bank. That would be a bit cooler to sit for a while," he suggested.

But the moment we got onto the field, I realized I had made a grave mistake. While Dada was well equipped in his sports shoes I had come in my slippers. Incessant rain for the last few days had converted the whole field into a mud pot. It was exceedingly difficult to make our way through the sticky soil. Half way down the field, I realized I had slowed down as he was at least a good fifty meters ahead of me.

"What's wrong, why are you lagging behind?" he shouted.

"It's my slippers, Dada, I should have come in my shoes."

"Take them off and walk bare foot. I am going ahead and will wait for you next to the banks." With this he disappeared behind the slope.

Bending down to take my slippers off, I realized I was standing exactly beneath the banyan tree. As I was trying to retrieve my slippers from the ankle deep mud, something touched my head, something heavy and cold. I froze. My senses told me that it could not be a branch, as the tree was quite tall and I had any which ways bent down. As I gathered enough courage to look up, what I saw chilled my blood in an instant. There hung from the branch the same dhoti clad man whom I had seen in the evening. Bare-chested, unshaved with unkempt white hair he hung there lifeless with his feet dangling in mid-air right above my head. The jolt on his neck had broken it as he stared down at me with eyes still open. A chill wind blew suddenly as the body started to swing. The weak rope lost its strength as it snapped....

I don't remember anything beyond this point. When I regained my consciousness, I was lying on the mud with my head on Dada's lap.

"Bapi, Bapi, what's wrong? What happened?" He sounded panicky as he splashed some water on my face.

"Dada, the dead man."

"What dead man? You have been imagining this dead man since evening."

I turned my head and looked up behind his head. There stood the loner with its outstretched arms. There was no sign of my tormentor. What hung from the same branch was a dirty white cloth, gently swaying in the soft breeze.

Decades have gone by since that fateful night. I have tried to rationalize the sequence of events multiple times with no effect. Still, today, I don't know what I saw and how I saw it. But the gallant Knight trotting proudly till then, decided to step down from his horse that very night. He walks now amongst the crowd shoulder to shoulder. No arguments, no debates.

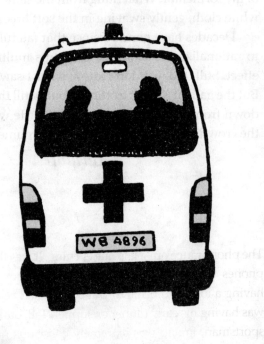

7

Antidote

I

The phone range quite late one evening. It was the land line. Mobile phones were only for the affluent class back then. Pratap, after having a long and tiring day at college had come back home and was having his early dinner or supper. Tall, dark, lanky and a born sportsman, Pratap was extremely conscious of his health. Come what may, he would get out of bed at five in the morning, even before the alarm would have ended and go out for his morning jog followed by his daily routine of weight training. He never preferred the gym. He found it too crowded. Running under the open sky and toning up muscles in his mini gym back home gave him most satisfaction. He was also very particular about his diet. Starting his day with a sumptuous breakfast, he would leave for college with his lunch pack from home. In the evening after getting home he would have his supper ensuring a gap of minimal four hours before hitting the sack. The world could have gone upside down but no one could lure him to eat any junk food in between these three meals, which he always wanted to have peacefully.

So when the phone rang, Pratap's mom, knowing her son too well picked up the phone without disturbing him. What followed after her saying hello was a dead silence at her end as she stood there motionless holding the receiver. Pratap's sharp sense told him something was wrong.

"What is it Ma?"

"He has done it again!" she replied in an icy tone after keeping down the receiver.

Pratap did not say a word. Without a hint of emotion or excitement he continued having his food. It took him five more minutes to finish his supper as he got up, washed his hands and went out of the house. It would be a five minutes walk round the next street.

"When would you be back?" asked his anxious mom.

"I am not sure Ma. Let me go and check the degree of damage this time. Don't wait for me, I might be late. I am carrying the house keys," with this he left like a breeze.

Pratap carried in him a maturity beyond his age. Level headed and cool it would take something unfair and unjust to make him angry. But if and when he got angry, people wanted to stay away from that zone for a while. That day while walking towards his destination he was fuming from inside. He knew he needed to control his wrath and was talking to himself as he entered the house.

The scene in the house where Pratap entered was beaming with histrionics all over. There were scores of people running here and there in panic as he heard loud noises coming from the mezzanine room to the right. As he entered that room, Arun's mom came and hugged him crying uncontrollably. Arun was sitting on a chair at one corner of the room, head down, blood oozing down from his head till his shirt, all drenched and brownish red. There were at least a dozen people in the room all trying to pacify him and make him understand something. Ashsihda, the doctor whom Pratap knew more as a brother was sitting helplessly in the other corner of the room.

"What is the matter?" Pratap asked in cold impassive voice.

"Pratap, he has been drinking since afternoon. In the evening he lost his balance and fell down the stairs. There is a big gash in his head and it needs immediate attention. Ashish has been trying to attend his wound since the last one hour but he would not let anyone go near him. Pratap, please do something," Arun's mom was hysterical.

Pratap pressed her shoulder gently and walked close to Arun's chair.

"Why are you not letting him attend your wound?" he asked in fiery baritone.

"I want my whiskey. They have hidden it. They are playing games with me Pratap," cried Arun.

What happened next was beyond anyone's wildest imagination. There was a loud sound followed by Arun flying off from the chair and falling in the ground as his specs went and landed on the doctor's lap. The well-toned muscular hand of Pratap had slapped Arun with all might. There was pin drop silence in the room as Arun tried to gather himself from the floor. One of Arun's sympathetic friends had started to approach him to lift him up.

"Don't even think about it," Pratap communicated looking into his eyes. "Everyone in this room leave now. Ashishda, come here and attend to the patient."

As the room got cleared without a single world of protest, Arun gathered himself and went back and sat on the chair. He did not retaliate even once. Crestfallen, he sat there speechless as the doctor inspected the injury.

"It's bad, will require stitches," he said.

"Go ahead Ashishda, do what is needed, he won't protest any more. I am around. Do let me know if you need my help," with this Pratap came out of the room permitting just one person to be there to assist the doctor.

He walked up to the terrace and lay down on the hammock. In a moonless sky the myriad diamonds tried in vain to glorify the Kolkata night sky. As the black expanse gently swung from one side to the other, Pratap felt like crying. His hand was paining from the force of the slap but that was bearable. What was beyond his limit of tolerance was the agony deep within. Few drops of warm saline dripped down his cheek as he drifted to the past.

Pratap and Arun went back fifteen years as friends. Next door neighbors, their first hug was as toddlers. Playmates to start with very soon they became inseparable soul mates. They went to the same school and progressed along life's path at the same pace never to let go each other's hand. By the time they passed out from school with the same grade, people would refer them as twins from the previous birth. Pratap wanted to become a Chemical Engineer while Arun a famous musician as he used to sing and play the guitar quite well for his age. The path was clear and they could see their goals when an unexpected incident hazed Arun's path. His dad passed away. Not even fifty, he didn't even leave an opportunity for Arun to hold his hand and say bye for the last time. Arun was shattered to say the least. Since that day Pratap could no longer find his old friend anymore.

With each passing day he got more and more submerged in abject grief and took to alcohol and smoking. Every other day he would get inebriated beyond his senses and create a scene at home. His mom left with no one but Arun never had the heart and courage to say anything to him. Pratap tried to bring him back to normalcy through multiple counseling, encouragement and love. But to his consternation things never improved.

The incident that just now happened was a vent out of Pratap's year old frustration while he had exhausted his entire repertoire to pull Arun back from the abysmal black hole.

"Pratap?"

Arun had come up to the terrace and was standing behind the hammock in bandaged shame.

Pratap hurriedly got up from the hammock and held his hand. "Are you nuts? Why did you come up in this state? Sit down here," Pratap was concerned.

"I am fine Pratap. Let me stand. The night is so beautiful isn't it?" he commented looking at the sky.

Pratap was quiet. He knew what Arun had to say. He would wait.

"I am sorry Pratap," a whisper was all that reached Pratap's ears. Pratap did not reply.

"I know, I know, I have done this multiple times and every time I shamelessly repeat my act. What to do Pratap? My misery is beyond me. Where is my fault you tell me? Whom did I harm to be punished like this?"

"Arun life is an accident. There is no pre life or after death. We all go through our shares of sorrow and joy. The time frame never matches making us believe we are the only tormented soul. So these questions that you ask yourself are rhetoric and will give you more soreness than relief. Get out of that grey world and be positive."

"Everyone is not as pragmatic as you Pratap. Life is not always black and white."

"Very well. So by sinking yourself in despondency and alcohol you think you can make your life colorful yet again?" a teetotaler himself Pratap hated anyone seeking solace in alcohol.

"You will never understand. Our path that we walked together a year back has bifurcated my friend, we have moved apart," Arun sighed.

Pratap sighed back and said, "OK for a moment let us believe there is afterlife. Do you think your dad, if he is seeing you from somewhere, would be euphoric to see you in this state? "

Arun was silent. He stared at the open sky, poignant.

"Let's go down, it's late and you need some rest," Pratap held his friends shoulder and gently walked him down the stairs.

Be it the shame of being slapped in public by his best friend or the words of rational wisdom shared by Pratap that night, Arun displayed a much rational and optimistic behavior in the days to come. Everyone was pleasantly surprised to see him stay away from alcohol or smoking. Arun's mom was the happiest of them all. She hugged Pratap the other day and held his hand crying uncontrollably.

"Pratap, thanks. I always knew only you could have cured him of this ailment. You have always been his role model, do you know that? He had told me so many times how he adores your disciplined and practical way of looking at life. You are exactly opposite to my son dear and your influence can and will heal his poor soul. Try and spend as much time as you can with him and bring him back from hell."

"Aunty, don't cry, please and don't thank me. I did and will do what I think is right for me to do for him. Talking about influence, well, if I were the cure then things would have got corrected long time back. He needs to realize from within and let's hope this time the jolt has given him enough food for thought," Pratap replied curtly holding her hand.

"It will, it most definitely will. I have always believed in your ability Pratap. You will do what me and my husband failed," she mumbled as she walked away from him.

Pratap felt embarrassed and stupefied to have been entrusted with such a big responsibility. But he was too rooted to the ground to be swayed by such expectations. He had seen too many such ephemeral remedial stages of Arun in the past one year. However, this time to his relief Arun continued to be quite normal beyond a month. He had attributed this to the self-realization of his friend when one day Arun walked into his house early in the morning.

"I think I am in love," blurted out Arun without any prelude with a sheepish smile.

Pratap was unflustered. He had been a neutral spectator to a plethora of amorous episodes of his friend since childhood to be reacting to this. Every other month his friend would get smitten by some mermaid round the corner and then would be chasing the mirage all day. He would be flying like a kite building castles in the air as Pratap would fruitlessly try to pull him back to reality.

"Pathetically predictable and boring you are my friend. I still don't know why we are such good friends," Arun would say and again fly back in the air.

"Who is it this time?" Pratap had a sarcastic smile on his face.

"Fatima," Arun was hardly audible.

"Who is Fatima? I hope you are not referring to the lady who stays next door to you?"

"Precisely Pratap, by the way don't address her as a lady, it sounds insulting," corrected Arun.

"Why of course, Fatima the girl in her sweet sixteen. Are you nuts Arun? She must be at least ten years elder to you! When will you ever be rational?" shouted Pratap.

"Ah! Knew it, you and your rationality. Where will it take you my friend? Have you ever thought what you gained through these self-inflicted shackles in your boring existence? Why do you have to judge an event even before it's born? Love is a river to swim and bathe in. You immerse in one point and reach some unknown destination. Don't sit on the bank Pratap, don't be so judgmental always in life. The day you finally decide to take a dip you might find the river dry!"

Pratap smiled, "Well, we all have our own beliefs and principles to hold on to. Nothing is right or wrong. Being righteous is to ensure a good sleep as the night falls. Anyway, now tell me about this girl. Is she equally smitten? Are you guys going along steadily for a while?" inquired Pratap.

"Well, actually no. I spoke to her for the first time yesterday as she had come to meet Ma," Arun was hesitantly honest.

"Wonderful, so now what's the plan?"

"You don't plan your love life, it happens," replied Arun with conviction in his voice.

"OK then, all the best for your happening dear. Let me know if you need my help. However, no one knows it better than you that I am the last person you should approach when it comes to an elixir for love." smiled Pratap.

II

"Pratap, rush to Arun without delay," Pratap's mom was standing anxiously in the garden near the front gate and shouted out as she saw her son walking back home from the college at the end of the day.

"What happened Ma?" asked Pratap tensed.

"He has done something gruesome, don't waste time, run," emphasized his mom.

Pratap handed over his college bag to her and started to run wondering all the way what could have happened. As he reached Arun's house and pushed his way up to his room amidst so many people, he was shocked to discover the morbid scene. The entire floor was a pool of blood as Arun lay on the bed half unconscious in pain. Ashishda was holding Arun's left arm over the elbow with all his might to prevent any further blood loss. Arun was in a state of intense shock and had the fear of death in his eyes. There was a faint sparkle as he saw Pratap. Arun's mom was hysterical praying to God to let her son live.

Pratap was next to Ashishda in a flash. Having judged the situation he knew exactly what needed to be done.

"How critical Ashishda?" he asked.

"Quite, he has cut the radial artery in his left hand with a blade. The blood loss is alarming. If we don't hospitalize him in the next thirty minutes, he cannot be recovered. I have already called for an ambulance; it should be here any minute."

"What about the police Ashishda? The hospital will ask for a police report!" Pratap's mind was working razor sharp.

"Don't worry; I will take care of that. It's my own hospital, I know the way around."

The siren was heard within minutes as Pratap and few others helped Arun get onto the ambulance. "You sit next to him Pratap and hold this place tightly, don't let any blood ooze out. We should be there within half an hour," instructed Ashishda.

Those thirty minutes in the Kolkata evening traffic was the longest half an hour in Pratap's life. He waited with bated breath as his friend still conscious looked at him with an expression of fear and guilt, tears flowing down his cheek.

"I am sorry Pratap. I should have listened to you. She never loved me. After a month of going around I got to know she was already engaged! Too immature to be mine was all she had to say as I asked her! Will I live Pratap?"

"Of course you will. Be positive, I am here with you, no one can harm you, you crazy fool, just stay with me," Pratap was almost in tears.

It took a bottle of Pratap's blood, six stitches, sedatives, Ashishda's personal relationship skills and a harrowing stormy night to get Arun out of danger. He was discharged the next day with few medicines and restrictions.

The next three months went by with Arun trying to handle the shame of a failed suicidal attempt. He became even more taciturn and cantankerous. He could never give up his addiction to alcohol and continued walking his path of eternal gloom. Pratap, utterly disgusted, sad and irate withdrew himself from his friend. A friendship which never ever saw a single day without them meeting and talking became frigid. During the initial recovery period he would go to Arun's place to enquire but post that he stopped. Ever positive, persistent and pragmatic Pratap had given up.

Two seasons went by with them not meeting each other. Both felt the same pain, both experienced the same void, both longed for each other to the same degree. Yet the crevasse grew wider waiting to be bridged as they both searched for pseudo solace beyond each other.

It was a hot afternoon as they accidentally met in front of Nandan Film Center. Pratap had gone there to watch the screening of digitally recovered Pather Pachali by Satyajit Ray when he saw Arun sitting on a bench. He was not alone. There was a girl sitting right next to him, with her head on Arun's shoulder. By the time Pratap saw both of them Arun had already seen him. There was no way the encounter could have been avoided, as desired by Pratap. Arun jumped up and came near Pratap. "How are you?" he asked as if they met yesterday.

"I am doing fine Arun, how are things with you?" Pratap, to his own revelation felt at ease.

"Breathing my friend, breathing.... Here, please meet my girlfriend Bipasha. We study together in the same college. Bipasha this is Pratap."

"Hi Pratap. Nice meeting you. I have heard so much about you that I feel I almost know you," said Bipasha enthusiastically as she greeted Pratap with an extended hand. Pratap smiled and looked at the girl. Yet another quixotic saga he pondered. His eyes fell on Arun's hand, the scar has not even healed, he thought. He indifferently looked beyond them to contemplate the turn of events and where his role would come in, a tragic end of course with him trying to pull back his friend from death. But he never let anything come on his face. Apologizing that he was getting late for the film he excused himself and gently walked away.

But this time Pratap's clandestine prophecy was falsified. More than six months went by and still Bipasha and Arun were in a relationship. Arun, no differently was head over heels for her while she was deeply in love with his artistic, musical and creative bent of mind. She knew his past and believed strongly that she could cure him of this depression through her love and care. A noble thought indeed and quite feasible had it not been for the pessimistic nature of Arun topped by his addiction to alcohol. After almost a year she realized that come what may she was unable to pull him out of his repeated feats of uncontrolled inebriation followed by his suicidal dips. Had she been not near him during those dark hours, yet another fatal occurrence would have happened. She did not give up but it was taking a heavy toll on her.

"Pratap, hurry, Arun needs you," Pratap's Ma had been yet again waiting anxiously for his son as he came back from the college.

"Again Ma?" was all he could mumble as he threw the bag to her and ran. Uncanny déjà vu he felt as he entered Arun's house expecting the repetition of yet another gruesome scene. As he rushed into the room expecting his friend to be lying on the ground surprised he was to find the scene had altered characters. The first person to rush to him hugging and desperately seeking help was not Arun's mom but Arun himself. The person lying on the bed half soaked in blood was none other than Bipasha, panic stricken, screaming for her life. The only unaltered character in the whole drama was poor Ashishda, again been called to attend this fatal fiasco.

Pratap had become a pro in suicidal disaster recovery. One exchange of glance between him and Ashishda and he knew exactly which pressure point to press and prevent the loss of blood. It was the left wrist this time, badly cut with a blade. Siren, ambulance, stitches, sedatives the sequence of events were identical with her recovering back to normalcy the next day. Two things differed this time. Pratap never had to give any blood as the loss was not that heavy and he intentionally made Arun sit inside the ambulance holding Bipasha's cut on the way to the hospital. Ashishda was not confident on this move but Pratap was adamant. He had a reason. He wanted Arun to face the petrified reflection of death in the eyes of his loved one.

III

Twenty years have gone by since that day. Arun and Bipasha are happily married and living a peaceful existence far away from Kolkata with their twin sons. The aspiration two teen friends had never bloomed as desired. Pratap never studied Chemistry. He is a successful investment banker instead. Arun works for the marketing division of a recognized firm. He still nurtures his dream of being a musician one day and looks at his sons for the fulfillment of his dream. After that traumatic incident when Bipasha had decided to end her own frustration of bringing back Arun from the eternal darkness by taking her own life, there was an astonishing change in Arun's behavior. He gave up his addiction completely and forced himself to look at the brighter side of life.

An unopened bottle of Glen Livet 21 and his old guitar both stand next to each other in his room, waiting to be picked up and dusted.

Arun's mom was wrong. An epitome of discipline, pragmatic Pratap was never the remedy to Arun's mental intoxication. The antidote was the toxin itself.

✦ ✦ ✦

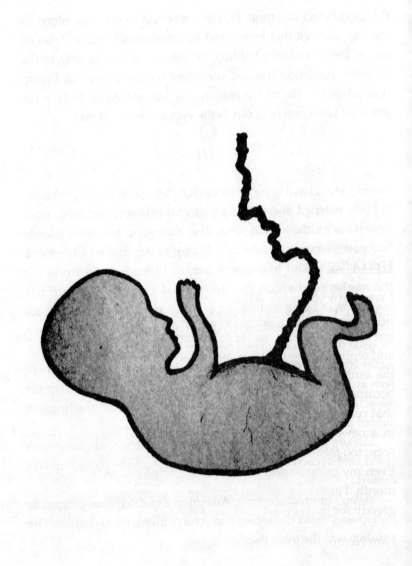

8

Memoirs of the Unborn

I was born yesterday. All of them were equally determined to fight this harsh world and reach my mom. They fought bravely but had to give their life for love. But my dad defied all hurdles and embraced her with his amorous love. Such passionate was the embrace that beyond the point their individual entities became non-existent, dissolved, relinquished for eternity. All that remained was a distant shadow and a faint remembrance in a newer individual. Thus I was born, too miniscule to be seen, too feeble to be heard, too unimportant to be attended to. Even my mom would not get to know of my arrival before a month. I am eager for that moment of acceptance, hungry and greedy for that special attention.

I am Nemo and this is my memoir.

31st Oct 2010:

As I get created cell by cell in the most amazing drama ever seen, I realize the only thing I am carrying from the past is my memory, a crystal clear, vivid and despairing representation of me dying alone in some remote corner of the world. It gives me shivers. I am glad I died. I am petrified to be reborn. So much suffering, so much of pain, such a circuitous path of joy and laughter, for what? I had achieved so much in life, had loved and revered so many, had been loved and revered by so many, had my share of benevolence and vengeance, had my quota of success and failure...but as I lay on my death bed desperately longing for a face whom I could relate to, as I had none, the futility of life dawned upon me. We talk about the wonders of the world and travel half the world to see and admire them. But if you ask me this is the biggest wonder of the world, the miracle of being reborn with all your memory erased as we are born with renewed hope to live.

20th Nov 2010:

She is not feeling well since morning as she is not able to eat anything due to nausea. I don't think she suspects my presence yet and believes her indisposition is due to regular food poisoning. When will she get to know? I am so anxious. I wish I had some ways to communicate to her, to let her know she is just inches away from her dream, heartbeat away from hope. I can't wait for the euphoric moment.

24th Nov 2010:

It's a black day for me. I am sad and have cried all day. My unformed eyes have got swollen and are paining. I am an unexpected, unwelcome guest, outcome of an accident, not love. It could not have been more painful. I wish I had not come back. She has been quiet and poignant all day. Is she even happy? I will never forgive him my entire life. The day my hands are formed I will strangle him and with tranquility, watch him die. While she was surprised, he was shocked to know. He shouted at her and accused her for being ignorant and careless.

"End this immediately. You know my social standing, I cannot take this responsibility. I will pay for everything, don't worry on the cost. It should be clandestine and clean." I could hear his voice like a rumble but he was loud enough even for my unformed ears to decipher.

25th Nov 2010:

She has been extremely quiet all day. Locked up in some place as dark as this, she has been sobbing all along. What is going in her mind? Will she play Prometheus or Anubis? I am vexed tonight. My unformed heart beats faster in anticipation. Will she or will she not let me be reborn? Do I or do I not get to return? Should I be happy or sad? I have so many questions tonight with answers unknown. I will try and sleep and hope for a brighter tomorrow.

30th Nov 2010:

I do not have words to express my happiness. In spite of all odds she has decided to embrace me. What a brave lady! My love and respect for her has touched the sky. Let me be born. She will never get to repent her decision. Her daughter will embrace her till eternity and not let a tinge of sadness touch her. He had come for the last time trying to convince her. He used up his entire repertoire of love, passion, force and threat to change her mind, but to no effect.

"I can't do it, its homicide. There are no accidents. If a life has come it must have come with a purpose. We are responsible for the happening and cannot shy away from it. I understand your anxiety and fear and hence won't force you into this. You are free to walk out. I will raise the baby alone. No one will ever know who the father is."

What a profound thought! What inspiring level of maturity at such a tender age? Where did she get so much of confidence? What makes her so strong? I want to grow up like her. I don't want a single gene from him to flow into me. I detest him. I have avenged in the past to my heart's content, I am waiting to do it again.

31st Dec 2010:

I have been growing steadily and miraculously each day. All my organs have formed to perfection waiting to grow in size. It was a big relief. I was quite worried. The last thing I wanted was to come back and be dependent on someone. I was no saint. Although I had kept my image clean, deep within I knew I had hurt many. A crooked dark side I had which was beyond my control. I paid the price in my lifetime as I waited eagerly to hold a known hand in my last hour. No one had come. Floating today in this placental abyss, I think I deserved such an end. But the sense of guilt and fear was still creating havoc in my mind. What if my karma would have got carried forward? How preposterous could it be to live a life wishing every moment not to live one, to suspect you are a reflection of your past yet be clueless as to what it was?

Today I can heave a sigh of relief.

24th Jan 2011:

It's not that I remember my entire past. They are like flashes appearing unexpectedly from nowhere making me laugh or cry. I remembered something today in the morning. I was claustrophobic all my life. I was trapped inside a closet while playing hide and seek with my sister when I was four. By the time my dad discovered me I was unconscious. I got back my consciousness but never got back my courage. Even taking the lift was an uphill task for me.

But look at me now! Trapped inside this dark cocoon with no space to stretch my arms and legs, connected to the outside world only through the umbilical cord, I should have been freaking to death by now. But what I feel is celestial bliss. A meditative stillness and assured protection that makes me wish for this world forever. Is it me who has changed? Or is it she who has made me change? I wish I knew.

6th Feb 2011:

Today is significant. She heard and saw me or the first time. At first I thought it was an earthquake as the noise came and hit me. Every molecule around me and I started shaking. I thought my last day had come. But soon the disturbance went down and I could hear her voice as she spoke to the doctor.

"She is so small doctor! Looks like an alien, so cute yet so fragile."

Alien? Did she just now refer me as an alien? I wanted to revolt and shout back in vehement objection. Well, my head might be a bit oversized compared to my body but that is because I am carrying so much of memory from the past!

"Yea, that's how babies look like after three to four months. Everything is normal, don't worry. By the way, don't be so sanguine about him or her. The stage of determination has not yet come and even when it comes you know the rules in our country."

"I know doctor. But I know it is her. I had always wanted a daughter and daughter she would be."

Tears flowed from my eyes. Liquid meeting liquid, not a drop lost. She knows I am here! She is waiting for me? Someone finally is waiting for me? In spite of what she went through she wants a daughter. This alien salutes you, Mom.

18th May 2011:

It's a fateful day for us. She fell down in the morning. The force hit me like an unannounced bomb as I was peacefully sleeping in my floating bed. I am still feeling a bit dizzy and everything around me looks hazy, as if my hydro microcosm has suddenly gone murky. She is also not well it seems as she might have injured her head too. I am praying for the well being of both of us.

19th May 2011:

We are better. Fortunately the injuries were superficial and none of us suffered any serious blow. She has been advised complete bed rest till the delivery date. There is not much time left. Another two months and I would get to see the light of the day. I am so excited and so is she.

21st July 2011:

The much awaited D day has finally come. I could not decide the time of my arrival. I wanted to, but my complicated posture, the cord's desperation to strangle me and my mom's diabetic constitution did not allow me to do so. It's going to happen tomorrow. It would be a very hectic day full of anxiety for both of us. Hence this would in all likelihood be my last memoir.

So Adieu my friends...tomorrow this time as you read my final scribble, I would have been reborn, completely oblivious of who I was. With all my precious and treacherous memory wiped out, I would be a clean slate, rejuvenated to face the drudgery yet again with magnified hope. Gone would be my past, gone would be these wonderful moments spent. I am certain the umbilical cord is my connection to the old world. Please doctor can you not cut it for me? Can you let me float in both the worlds?

I died a painful death to be born again. This is the final moment as I part with all my memories, good or bad. I sign off my memoir, pregnant with optimism that the new birth would shower me with infinite happiness.

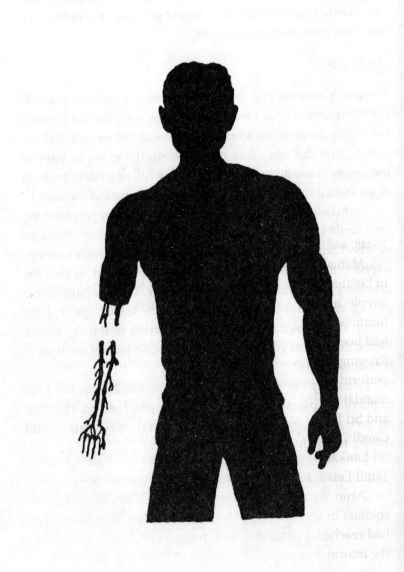

9

Phantom

"Saab, andar maat jao."

Mange Ram shouted with all his might to draw the attention of Lieutenant Arun Joshi who was about to enter a dilapidated temple in the middle of a dense forest in some undisclosed location in Sri Lanka. Arun along with his Grenadiers battalion, had been deployed to Sri Lanka as a part of the Indian Peace Keeping Force which was the Indian military contingent performing peacekeeping operations in Sri Lanka under the mandate of the Indo-Sri Lankan Accord signed between India and Sri Lanka in 1987. The aim of Indian Prime Minister Rajiv Gandhi was to end the Sri Lankan Civil War between militant Sri Lankan Tamil nationalists lead by the Liberation Tigers of Tamil Eelam (LTTE) and the Sri Lankan military.

Arun had been leading his entire team of exceptional soldiers in a combing operation for the last four hours. They had reached a particular spot in the forest where according to the information received, a group of five to six LTTEs had put up a temporary shelter. The information was immaculate. They took the militants by surprise and put down three even before they realized the danger. However, the other three escaped into the denser forest as Arun started chasing them. LTTEs were masters of the guerilla warfare and would mix with the thick foliage so proficiently that even a person standing within touching distance would not realize the presence. Yet after hours of chasing and cross firing, Arun with his team could gun down two of them. One of his jawans got critically hit and could not accompany any further. Arun asked the troops to be with him and fearlessly continued chasing the last militant. His Junior Commissioned Officer, Mange Ram would have never let him go alone. He checked his ammunition supply for the sten machine carbine and followed Arun like a shadow. After about half an hour of relentless search, Mange Ram detected a sudden movement up on a tree hundred yards at three o'clock. He immediately fired. A desperate cry and loud thud indicated he had hit the target. As they ran towards the tree they could see a blood trail leading them further north. Not a single word was shared between the two as they glanced at each other and started following the trail. Within five minutes they suddenly reached an open area where the decrepit temple stood. The militant had most definitely taken that shelter. By then Arun was throbbing in excitement and wanted to finish the job quickly. It was then that he ran towards the temple door impetuously; Mange Ram shouted warning him not to enter. His more than twenty years of service and erstwhile experience in such guerrilla warfare told him to be extra careful.

The sequence of events to follow in the next three minutes would change Lt. Arun Joshi's life drastically. It would be a turning point in his career and bring in him a dramatic change.

Arun was born to a family which breathed the Indian Army. His grandfather had fought the war of 1971 and heavy with medals, awards and pride retired as the Vice Chief of the Army. His father commanded the same Grenadiers battalion in which Arun was commissioned, parental claim as they say, while his elder brother had already lived up to the expectation by qualifying for the Defence Services Staff College with only nine years of service. So when Arun got into the Indian Army, it was but obvious that he would do well. Excelling in the military seemed to be in his blood as even as a cadet he started demonstrating amazing physical and intellectual capability. Within six months of his getting commissioned he went for the commando training and as he walked out as the Commando Dagger topping the batch, everyone knew he had taken off in his family tradition. Boiling with uncontainable energy, stooping with self-created expectation, burning with aspiration and glowing with overconfidence, Arun believed he could win the world. He had to reach the top and he had to do it fast.

So when his JCO shouted '*Saab andar maat jayo*' he ignored the warning. Before Mange Ram could react, he was inside the temple firing relentlessly from his carbine. The temple had a central courtyard and small enclosures all across. His sharp sense told him that the militant must have taken shelter in the remotest corner. The blood trail also confirmed the same. He never stopped spraying the bullets as he entered the small room. His suspicion was flawless. There lay on the floor a young lad, still in his teens, critically wounded, bleeding heavily and breathing his last. What the foolhardy Lieutenant had not taken into calculation was the suicidal nature of these guerrillas. Arun realized to his horror that the lad had already opened the pin of a grenade and was holding it in his hand looking straight into his eyes with a sarcastic smile.

Once the pin is removed a grenade takes four to five seconds to blast.

All Arun remembered was a deafening noise as he desperately tried to jump away from the blast site. Then it was a dark abysmal crevasse.

When Arun regained consciousness in the Army Hospital in Chennai, three days had gone by. He had been flown out of Sri Lanka immediately after the blast. It took eight grueling hours of surgery to save him. The blast of the grenade at such close quarters had taken a heavy toll on him.

Arun survived, but had to pay the price with his hand.

Disfigured beyond repair, his right hand had to be amputated below the elbow. His leg could be saved but he would be having a limp all his life. The right half of his face had a heinous scar.

Arun was devastated. Traversing at an accelerated speed towards glory, all it took was his split second overconfidence and a hand grenade to shatter his dreams.

When his Commanding Officer walked into the hospital to pay him a visit after a week, he could barely sit up on the bed.

"How are you doing my son?"

"Good morning Sir. I am doing better thank you," replied Arun sharply.

"Son, I am sorry for what has happened to you. I know it would take you some time to accept this, but we will take care of your career. You should have listened to Mange Ram. It's sad Arun, you were one of the best officers in making. Take care and get well soon."

With this the Commanding Officer gently squeezed his good hand and marched out along with his entourage. His words 'you were one of the best officers in making' echoed in the room long after he left. Arun realized that he was already been referred in the past tense. The Indian Army had branded him as a falling star about to dissolve away in the oblivion.

His brother and dad were sitting next to him with their heads down. He knew that he had failed them too.

When Shweta walked in with a bouquet, the expression on her face was more of shock than sadness. One look at her and Arun knew his yet another dream had shattered. Neither she nor her parents called to cancel the marriage. A small box containing the solitaire engagement ring arrived as a courier. There was not even a courtesy note.

Injured on duty, Lt. Arun Joshi, was transferred to Ordinance. A desk job with a guaranteed salary at the end of each month and pension till death, he knew he would be soon forgotten. He felt like a hollow man from inside. The merciless doctor had amputated his soul. His heaviness grew each day to the point of contemplating suicide. He was at his tethers end and could take the pain no more. Least did he know that the worse was still awaiting him.

The attack came in the middle of the night, exactly two months from the dreadful encounter. The excruciating pain was so intense that he woke up in a shock. His wounds had all healed. What were left were the embarrassing scars and the stunted limb. The pain was coming from his right side. Initially he thought that the post amputation pain had returned for some reason. But then to his shock and horror he realized the pain was in his right hand. The point of genesis was his right forearm and went down till his thumb. It was a throbbing agony with an intensity he had never ever experienced before. Arun was flabbergasted. He could not believe his eyes. How could he get a pain and that too so intense and real in his right hand which was no longer a part of his body! Discarding it as a surreal figment of his imagination, he got up and splashed some water on his face. His drowsiness left him but not his agony. Desperate to get rid of the discomfort, he even took a pain killer but with no effect. No pain killer could have cured a pain which was outside his body. Arun had no option but to bear it and wait for it to automatically subside. He had tears in his eyes as he sat at the corner of his room, head within his knees, his left hand grasping his right limb with all his might. It took more than an hour for the pain to go away, leaving the Lieutenant depressed and stupefied.

Next morning as he woke up, it all seemed like a nightmare. He laughed at his own stupidity and continued with the day as usual. Still trying to learn the art to survive using just his left hand, Arun Joshi completely forgot about the bizarre incident all throughout the day. He had still not remembered it when he went to bed in the night.

It struck him again exactly at midnight and this time it came back with a vengeance. He was terrified as he again took refuge in one corner, writhing in pain, helplessly waiting for it to pass away. This time he clocked it. Exactly fifteen minutes past one o'clock it disappeared as abruptly as it had come.

Arun decided to go to the Hospital next day and consult Col. Rathore, an old hand in Orthopedics.

"Yes Lieutenant, how are you doing?" warmly welcomed the doctor.

"Thank you Sir. Honestly, I am not sure how am I doing," replied back Arun.

The Colonel was inquisitive. "What do you mean son?"

"Well, on one hand is the overall recovery from the trauma where I think I have jumped back fine. But on the other hand I have started experiencing an unbearable pain in the night." Arun was skeptical.

"Pain as in?" the doctor was eager.

"I don't know how to say Sir but it is in my right hand, starting in the forearm and ending in the thumb," blurted out Arun.

"What are you saying? How on earth is that possible Lieutenant? I am sorry to say, but your right arm has been amputated and incinerated more than two months back. You cannot have pain in that part of your body which is not there." Shouted the doctor.

"I know Sir. But how can I disregard the severe agony when it comes and hits me in the night?"

"Sorry son. I cannot give you medicine for this. Why me, no doctor can. It's all in your mind. The faster you can come to terms with the void limb faster you would be out of this," concluded the Colonel.

Arun was disoriented and dubious. The doctor's nonchalant dismissal of his predicament made him feel quite silly. Uncertain, he jumped back in the day to keep his mind occupied, hoping that the night would be peaceful. That night he could not go to sleep as he waited with trepidation for the dark hour. He stared at his non-existent right hand to make himself believe that there was no hand. He clung to the faint ray of hope with his single hand, expectant. As the old fashioned wall clock struck twelve, the ghost announced its appearance again in the same uncanny way. It came, devastated and exited in a planned way, punctual and methodical as ever.

Arun got paranoid. He started believing that during the blast, few splinters must have got into his skull and affected the brain to make it function abnormally. He was convinced he was losing his mind. Nervous, he decided to visit the Psychiatrist at the Army Hospital.

As he explained his case to Capt. B. Basu, a young lady in the Psychiatry Department, she was intrigued. To Arun's relief she did not dismiss him like the Colonel.

"You are suffering from Phantom Limb syndrome Lieutenant. It is the sensation of an amputated or missing limb still attached to the body when in reality it is not. Approximately 60 to 80 % of individuals with an amputation experience phantom sensations in their amputated limb, and the majority of the sensations are painful. Till date no one has been able to convincingly explain the reason for the same and it remains yet another mystery of the human brain. Since the cause is unknown, there is no cure too. I am sorry Lieutenant; I can't do much to help you in this. You can try and train your mind and impose self-conviction on the absence of the same. That can help."

Arun did not know how to react. He was caught between the rock and the hard place. On one hand he was relieved to know that he was not the only lunatic being tormented by his missing limb. But on the other hand he was equally disturbed to know that this apparent madness had no cure. The very thought of bearing the pain for the rest of his life made him shiver within.

The phantom never left him. In fact it got worse with time. After each attack, Arun would sit back alone in his room and cry. An atheist and a staunch non believer in karma, he would wonder for what he was being punished this way. Everyone had deserted him in the recent past. His pride, career, aspiration, glory, fiancée, looks, all had abandoned him just like a child dumps his most precious toy once the transient interest is gone. As if that was not enough, his mind was now playing games with him mocking and reminding him of his loss each night.

He could not take it anymore. He decided to end his life and he would have most definitely done so had it not been for Kanika.

They met in the local park in a winter morning. Arun, despondent to the core and seriously contemplating how to end his suffering was sitting alone in one corner of a bench, poignant and distant from this world.

"Do you mind if I sit here?" A young girl in her mid-twenties was standing next to Arun looking at him with a benevolent smile.

Arun was surprised and looked back to check whether she was addressing someone else. In the past one year since that dreadful day, people had all gradually moved away from him. People would cringe and look away while children cried and ran for their parents. It would hurt him even more than the phantom pain.

So he was perplexed to see this lady trying to talk to the scar faced one handed demon.

"Sure you can," whispered Arun.

"Hi, I am Kanika. I live in that blue two storied building that you see across the street? I see you every day taking a walk in this park or sitting by yourself on this bench. I hope you don't mind if I talk to you?"

Tall, fair, with thick black hair flowing down her knees and large innocent benevolent eyes which could melt the darkest soul, Kanika looked like an Angel in the morning light.

Arun looked at her and smiled as she continued to talk without any pause. Kanika was a compulsive communicator. Human mind has a barricade between thought and communication, a barricade that stops us from chattering till infinity. Kanika was born without that barricade. Thus the one sided conversation went on for the next half an hour with Arun listening to her endless drone with rapt attention. It was after a long time that someone had sat in front of his distorted self and spoken at length. He was touched.

"Oh my God!" Kanika exclaimed looking at her watch. "I had to get eggs for Mom, Dad had to leave for office." With this she jumped out of her seat and ran towards the grocery store across the street. No bye, no apologies for being abrupt, no looking back at him while running. She came and went like a tempest. But Arun was not hurt. On the contrary, he was quite amused. As he got up and started walking away from the park he was surprised to feel a hint of optimism taking birth in his void soul. He could never say what it was, but he wanted to come back the next morning to the park.

As Arun waited on the bench next morning with confused expectations, Kanika did come. This time it was even more abrupt. She just walked from behind the bench, sat and started the conversation as if the one full day in between had not even come.

"I hope you have bought the eggs before coming here," Arun joked.

"Eggs? What eggs?" Kanika had surprise on her face.

"Never mind, please continue." Arun smiled as Kanika continued explaining how upset she was with her pet cat.

Thus their friendship continued to grow each day. Each day they would laugh and cry together, each day they shared myriad moments with each other, each morning they would eagerly wait for the sun to rise to meet each other. In two months it seemed they knew more about each other than their own parents. Arun even visited her place and was amazed to find a similar kind of acceptance from her parents too. He had started to develop a warm feeling towards her and wanted her to be with him forever. However, he was dubious about her feelings. After all, he was what he was, a somber shadow from the past. How could he expect a beauty like Kanika to even think anything beyond friendship with him? He convinced himself that he should not be greedy and accept her as his well-wisher and an intimate friend.

The unexpected happened well within six months of their knowing each other on a Sunday evening as they were taking a stroll in the park.

"Are you serious about me?" asked Kanika looking straight into Arun's eyes.

Arun was shocked and looked away.

"What do you mean?" he asked avoiding her eyes.

"You know what I mean. Look into my eyes and answer me."

Arun did not know how to react. He just mumbled, "Kanika, don't be a kid. This is not yet another whim and fancy of yours."

Kanika stopped abruptly on the path and looked at him, deeply hurt. Arun was still looking away. By the time he gathered enough courage to look, she was gone. He did not make any attempt to call her back and slowly left for his home.

Two days went by in a state of acute morbidity for Arun as he withdrew himself in his cocoon. He never got out of his room and sat in dark solemn introspection. He had not expected this. Having wished for this to happen every moment he had equally dreaded the hour.

There was a desperate knock on the door followed by repeated ringing of the doorbell. As Arun slowly went and opened the door, Kanika entered like a whirlwind.

"Why are you avoiding me? Why have you not come to the park for the last two days? Why are you treating me as if you don't love me? What is wrong with me?" bombarded Kanika relentlessly.

"Kanika, relax, have a seat first. It's not about you. Nothing is wrong with you, you are just perfect. It would be my dream come true to have you by me. But you need to realize that this is a decision you cannot take impetuously. Look at me! An invalid Lieutenant with no future, that's who I am Kanika. On top of that I doubt my mental stability too. I have never ever shared with you, but I have this unbearable phantom pain in my right forearm. No Kanika, I don't want to ruin your life," Arun was almost in tears.

"That's it?" asked Kanika surprised. "Is that the only reason for which you have been running away?"

Arun had by then taken his seat at the end of his bed. Kanika slowly came and sat next to him and touched his hand. She bent down to lift her sari, disengaged her Jaipur foot and kept it in front of Arun.

"You are not alone in this world Arun, we all have our own battles to fight."

The phantom made an unexpected return. But this time Arun felt it somewhere close to his heart.

10

Intrepid

Bibek Lahiri was a self-made man. Tall, handsome, witty and full of exuberance he had reached the pinnacle of his career at a very early age. Hovering in his mid-thirties and already the Vice President of a renowned international bank, he was the blue eyed boy of the higher management and envy of many others under the same roof.

Born and brought up in the outskirts of Kolkata, Bibek lost his dad to a road accident on an ill-fated day when he was just ten years old. His mother, a government servant, somehow managed to raise him bearing acute hardship without a cringe on her face. When after a long day, she would lie down on the bed canopied by the mosquito net and writhe in pain, Bibek would massage her feet in spite of her vehement objection. As his little hands would gradually take away her pain to make her drift to a world of dreams and the soft light from the street lamp would fall on her face through the window, making her look like an Angel, Bibek would curse their luck. 'Why it had to be his Dad? Why this misery had to befall them? Why his mom couldn't live an average peaceful life of no hardship?' The dead silence of the night punctuated by the barking of the dogs and the relentless yet sincere whistle of the security guard would have no answer for him. However, deep down him, developed an intense apathy and hatred towards Providence and Destiny. As he would see his mom bend down in front of countless idols all carefully placed on a stool at one corner of the room, as she would follow all rituals and religious doctrines meticulously, he would ask his mom, "Whom are you paying respect to Ma and for what? Believe me, it's just us left to ourselves to manage this world. There is no Supreme Being. If He was there; you would not have been driven through this acid test for no apparent fault of yours!"

To this his mom would dreadfully reply, "Don't say such things Bibek. You should never disrespect Him."

"Oh, come on Ma! I don't fear anyone. I will show you one day that you can be successful in life on your own capability. You don't have to fear or respect any ulterior force. I will Ma, carve my own destiny and you will see it with your own eyes one day." bragged Bibek.

So he vowed and so he did. A brilliant student from his very childhood, he topped the IIT entrance exam to get an engineering seat in Electronics at IIT, Kharagpur. His feats did not end there. As he was in his final semester he topped CAT to get into IIM, Joka. As he passed out from Joka with a MBA degree in business finance, all big investment banks and corporate were standing at his doorstep with unthinkably lucrative offers. He accepted an offer in one of the topmost financial firms and moved out of his native state along with his Mom to settle down in the capital.

His intelligence, smartness and presence of mind backed him in the corporate world too as he rose like a star in the years to come. Changing two jobs in ten years when he completed a decade in this rat race, he was married to Sneha with a five year old son Ritwik.

Life's course had inflated Bibek's ego to a perilously high level. It had reached the red level marked in the dam beyond which you knew the tumultuous water would overflow anytime and wash away all traces of tranquility across miles. People around sensed and preempted the obvious, but he never had those inner pair of lenses to realize the same. Thus it continued as he achieved more and more fame each year.

Sneha, his wife, was an exact opposite. Soft spoken, homely, down to earth and deeply religious she was a perfect homemaker. Their son, Ritwik, was also a very well behaved and understanding child. While Bibek was much focused as to how to make his son successful in this competitive world, Sneha would be more interested to make a good human being out of him. The little kid was very attached to his grand mom, as beyond the world of eternal parental expectations she was his only solace. A place where he could walk into and just be what he wanted to be with no questions asked.

The life changing incident for Bibek happened on 31st of October, a day celebrated all across the world as Halloween. Hallows' Eve is a yearly celebration dedicated to remembering the dead, including saints, martyrs and all the faithful departed believers. People across the world, primarily children dress themselves up in weird and gory costumes as if they have risen from their graves to scare off each other. Till a few years back this would only be celebrated in the western countries. However, with the world getting smaller every day, India had also got infected with this fever.

Ritwik, for some unknown reason developed an inexorable affinity towards Halloween. He caught this from his condominium friends and all of them decided to dress up as human skeletons on that day. So he approached his mom with his request, "Ma, can you get me a human skeleton dress for this Halloween? The one that glows in the dark?"

Sneha was a bit surprised but replied, "Oh My God! Why do want to scare all of us sweetheart? Why can't I get you a less scary dress?"

"Mom!!! Its Halloween, not my birthday! The motif is to scare people. Please Ma," pleaded Ritwik.

"Okay, okay don't be dramatic, I will get you one. When is this Halloween of yours?"

"It's tomorrow Mom," replied the kid in a matter of fact way.

"Tomorrow? And you are telling me now? Couldn't you have told me a few days earlier? Now I have to ask your Dad to get it on his way back from office and you know how busy he always is!" Fumed Sneha.

"Please ma, I know you will make this happen as always. There is one more thing...."

"Now what??"

"I want dad also to celebrate this day with me."

"As in?" asked Sneha perplexed.

"I want him to also wear the dress and be with me tomorrow evening," calmly answered Ritwik.

"Rit, have you gone completely out of your mind? You know your dad right? Convincing him to get this dress for you would be a task and on top of that you expect him to come home early from office and roam around dressed like a human skeleton inside this complex? Let's be rational here Rit," logically explained Sneha.

To this little Rit, did not reply and left the room crestfallen. Sneha knew from where he was coming. She exactly understood the poor kid's deep rooted psychology. Bibek was ever busy and was hardly there as a dad when he needed him. Even over the weekends when the little boy would wait with great expectation for his dad to come and play with him, Bibek would either be traveling or be in office or taking calls from home. Sneha would try her level best to fill in the gap. She would accompany him every day to the park and spend as much time with him as she could. But as a boy, when he kicked the football, swung the bat, sprinted across the park or rolled on the mud the one and only entity he missed next to him was his Dad. Sneha could sense that void gradually building up and had tried talking it out with Bibek. It was not that Bibek didn't care. It was just that he was so deeply trapped in his own race that he couldn't manage any time beyond that.

Sneha sighed and picked up the phone. It was half past two. Typically Bibek would be having his lunch.

"Bibek, busy?"

"Was quickly finishing my lunch, Sneha. Have to rush to a marathon meeting in fifteen minutes. Tell me, anything urgent?"

"Well, yea. We have a situation here. Ritwik wants to celebrate the Halloween tomorrow and he just now told me he needs a glowing human skeleton dress. You know Bibek, I can't go and get it today, so was thinking would it be possible for you to pick one up on your way back?" communicated Sneha reluctantly.

"Sneha!!! This is ridiculous. You know how busy I am right? I have meetings till eight. By the time I leave office all shops would be closed. Sorry Dear, I can't," said Bibek bluntly.

"Bibek, please, do something. He is waiting with a lot of expectation," pleaded Sneha.

Bibek sighed. "OK text me the details. Let me try online and get it delivered by tomorrow morning."

"Thanks. There is one more thing." Whispered Sneha fearfully.

"Now what?" shouted Bibek looking at his watch.

"He wants you to celebrate this festival with him," said Sneha expecting a tempestuous reaction from him.

"As in me dressed like a glowing human carcass and making a fool of myself in public? Sneha, I think we are going a bit too astray here. I am getting late. Send me the details. Let me see what I can do."

With this Bibek abruptly disconnected the call. *'Have they lost their sanity? Both mother and son? Do they realize what they are expecting from me? This is the most ludicrous proposition I have ever come across in my life!!!'* Bibek glanced at his watch and realized he still had few minutes before the meeting would start. Sneha had already texted the details. So he went online and quickly ordered the dress. He cringed as fifteen hundred rupees drained immediately through his pocket. Twenty four hours guaranteed delivery or money back they said.

Next day early morning as Bibek was having his morning tea and leafing through the newspaper, Ritwik came and sat next to him quietly. His bobbing head could be seen over the newspaper as Bibek smiled and said, "Good Morning Rit. How are you doing today? Are you not getting late for school?"

"Good Morning Papa. No I have ten minutes before the bus comes," replied the boisterous chap.

"Papa, when will my dress arrive?"

"Well, it should be here before you are back from school dear. Don't worry," assured Bibek.

"Thanks a lot Papa. And can you also please...," requested Ritwik with trepidation. But before he could complete the sentence Bibek said, "Look son, I know where you are going. Let me be very candid so that you don't dwell in unrealistic expectation and then feel hurt. I won't be able to come home early today and celebrate this day with you. There are two reasons to that. One obviously is because I have meetings till late night. The second is something I want you to listen very carefully and absorb," conveyed Bibek.

"Do you know son, why this day is celebrated?"

"To celebrate the dead I presume. But for me it's the fun of being dressed so weird and scaring people," was his innocent reply.

"Well, to an extent you are right. But there is a very deep rooted psychological reason behind celebrating this day. As humans we all have our own fears. Fears we struggle all our lives to overcome, dreads we all run away from till we die. It is believed that the only way you could overcome that terror is to face it head on. Based on this principle people embrace their deadliest horror and dress up like that hoping that once faced and embraced it would leave them forever," lectured Bibek as Ritwik listened eagerly.

"So let me ask you son, what is your greatest fear?"

"Cockroaches dad, I hate them!" Exclaimed Rit.

"Well, ideally you should have been dressed like one today. But it's a little too late for that. Maybe you can give it a thought next year. And now ask me what is my biggest fear?"

"What is your biggest fear Papa?"

"None," was Bibek's blunt reply.

"Which demon is None Papa?"

"It is no demon my son, none as in nothing. I have no fear within me. I lost my dad when I was little older than you. I saw so much hardship your grandma had to go through. Life was never fair to us, but yet I struggled and reached here, fearless and victorious. I have neither believed nor feared either God or Destiny my son forget about any lesser mortals. So you see, the basic principle of celebrating Halloween is not applicable to me. And now, you are really getting late for school. Rush, else you will miss the bus."

Enlightened, confused and still sad Ritwik slowly started his journey towards the bus stop holding his mom's hand as Bibek again got busy with his daily news.

"How much it would have taken, Bibek, to listen to the little chap? Is it always necessary to be so hung up in life?" asked his Mom, as she was sitting very close by all along listening to the entire conversation.

"Let's not start it all over Ma. I don't have time for this," he replied irritated and left the room.

The mobile rang exactly at 7.30 p.m. Bibek was deeply engrossed in a financial planning meeting when Sneha's name flashed on the screen. Instinctively, he disconnected. Within seconds it again flashed with the same name. Now this worried Bibek. Generally as a routine she would know that he was in a meeting and would wait for him to give a ring back.

"Excuse me gentlemen, I need to take this call," he apologized as he stepped outside the meeting room.

"Yes, what is it?" asked Bibek with concerned irritation.

"Rit is missing!" shouted Sneha alarmed.

"What do you mean he is missing? He must be around. There is no way he could have gone outside the complex. Have you checked with his friends? He must be in one of his friend's house!"

"Bibek, I have been doing all that since the last one hour. I would not have given you a call otherwise. He is not with any of his friends. He was last seen playing with his friends in the park dressed up in his Halloween dress. No one has seen him after that. All my friends in this complex have already started searching. Could you come down please? I am awfully worried."

"I will be there right away dear, you continue the search and just hold on," hurriedly replied Bibek as he entered the meeting room and declared, "I am sorry folks, I have an emergency and have to leave."

Without even waiting for anyone's response he left the office and started driving back. It was usually a thirty minute drive home late in the night when he would leave office. But today he was confronted with the regular office rush and realized it would take him close to an hour to reach home. Bluetooth on, he called Sneha, "Any news?"

"No. We are still searching. I have inquired at the main gate. The security guards are sanguine he has not left the complex."

Fifteen minutes down the line he again called hoping that she would give her the good news.

"No, still nothing Bibek. We are going through the video footage in the CCTV to see where he was last seen. Till now no trace. When are you coming?"

"I am cursing the traffic. It's moving like a snail. This is extremely frustrating. I think I will take another thirty minutes before I reach."

Bibek could feel the blood pressure building up as his temples started throbbing. He could almost hear the sound. The FM jockey was chatting away to frivolous glory to irritate Bibek even more. He switched off the radio and thought hard. 'Where could he have gone? Ritwik was a very well behaved and obedient child. He would not wander off just like that. He always told his Mom where he was going and got back home on time. Where did he vanish then? Has some one kidnapped him? Drugged him, put him inside the car and taken him away? Or maybe someone whom he knew very well duped him with a false promise and took him away? The guards were definite that he had not left the complex. But how much could you actually trust them too? In this dark world where you would only get to read news of rape, child abuse and abduction across the front page whom actually could you trust?'

Bibek could feel his palms sweating as all these disturbing thoughts came and haunted his mind. By the time he reached the parking of his apartment complex, it was almost 9.30 p.m. He could see the police van parked in front of their building. They were asking everyone routine questions.

Seeing Bibek, Sneha came running in and hugged him. "I had to call the police Bibek. It's been more than three hours now and we have no trace! It seems he has vanished without a trace. Even the video footage doesn't have him."

Till now Bibek was riding on his hopes that by the time he reached home, they would have found him. In spite of all the sinister thoughts clouding his mind, he still was optimistic. But now having seen the police his legs gave way. He sat down at the park bench holding his head. Ritwik's despondent look as he left for the school, his innocent plea to dance with his dad both dressed like ghostly clowns, his large soft ever inquisitive eyes pierced him like an arrow that evening.

His unfinished request, "Thanks a lot Papa. And can you also please...," reverberated all around him like a whirlwind sucking the last ray of hope from him.

"Don't lose hope Bibek." Sneha was sitting next to him holding his hand. "He will come back to us unscathed. I have complete trust in Him. I have never ever harmed anyone, come what may my son would be safe," uttered Sneha with innermost conviction and belief.

Bibek looked up to her with surprise. 'How come she had so much trust on someone so abstract and yet be so hopeful? Even in turmoil like this she has the faith to hold on?'

"Papa!!!"

Both Bibek and Sneha were startled to hear their son's voice from behind. They jumped from the bench to see Ritwik gleefully walking towards them dancing in joy all dressed up in his glowing suit blissfully unaware of the tension all around.

"Rit, where were you? Where had you gone? We have been searching for you for the last four hours!!!"

Within seconds the entire crowd realized that the child was found and loomed around him to ask hundred questions.

Ritwik was petrified. He realized that he must have done something wrong. With a quivering voice he replied to his mom, "I was playing at Krishna's place Ma."

"Who is Krishna? I have never heard about this friend of yours? Where does he stay? Why didn't you inform me?" bombarded Sneha.

"Krishna is my new best friend Ma. They have arrived here from Mumbai two days back. I was playing Halloween games with him and both of us were dressed the same. So I went to his apartment and started playing," replied Rit innocently.

"I can't believe this," screamed Bibek. "Where were his parents when we were searching for you for the past four hours? How dare you be so ignorant of time? Haven't I told you a hundred times to get back home before the sun sets? Do you think we are fools trying to hunt you out since evening?"

"His parents had to go out early in the evening and asked us to continue playing Papa. I am sorry, I read the wall clock wrong," replied the child in tears.

"Don't scold him anymore Bibek. Let's go home. Thanks all of you, we are extremely sorry for putting all of you through this."

Relieved Sneha hugged Ritwik and took him away from the crowd inside the home.

As the red-wattled Lapwing gave out its shrill alarm call to announce the end of the drama, as a disturbed lone Raven cawed somewhere up in the tree, as the Barn owl heaved a sigh of relief for having finally got its focus back on the prey, the only person still left behind on the scene was Bibek.

He sat quietly on the same bench drenched in mixed emotions. His hands were shaking, he was breathing heavily.

Even in a late October Delhi evening, his shirt was sodden. He could not remember for how long he was there. Time seemed warped to him that evening. He slowly got up and went back home. Thinking a cold splash of water would help him regain composure, he went to the washroom. As he was about to splash water on his face, he was horrified to see his own face. The person staring back at him was not the egocentric Bibek Lahiri anymore. Hair all unkempt, cheek sunken, dark shadow under his eyes and a reddish complexion, he looked to have won the Halloween dress competition that evening. He smiled and went to peep in Rit's room. Tired, afraid and fossilized he had slept off in his skeleton clothes even without having dinner. Bibek slowly sat next to him and touched his head as tears flowed down his cheeks. Inadvertently his little menace had succeeded in making him participate in the Halloween evening.

Intrepid Bibek Lahiri was glad to be afraid....

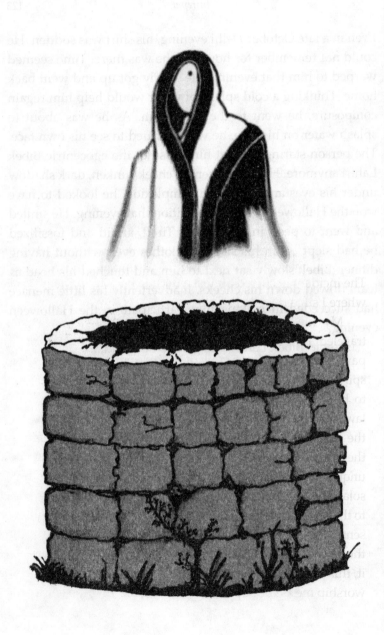

11

Liberation

The incident occurred almost a decade back in the same house where I sit and write this story.

My life has been an interesting journey where I have traveled across India meeting all kind of people from the pauper to the King. I have led two distinct existences of spirituality and materialism and I believe I have done justice to both. My wife, children, grandchildren and daughter-in-law have no room for complaint as they enjoy the luxury of the wealth I have accumulated through my entire life. On the other hand I have also nurtured my spiritual life with unquestioned dedication. That is where I have always found solace beyond my perfunctory material existence. Maybe due to this dual existence of mine or because of my own heightened sensitivity, I have had experiences all my life which are beyond the power of our rational mind to comprehend. If I share all of it, this pragmatic world would either put me on a podium and worship me as the supernatural or tag me an imposter to mock me. I have inclinations towards none and hence have kept quiet most of my life. Very few people have been made privy to my paranormal world but those limited few are and will always remain very near and dear to me. It is because of the request of one of them that I have no option but to pen down this particular incident today. He is the only other person till date who knows this incident in my life. Sitting down and writing about my own life is the last thing I would do given my lazy and indifferent attitude towards life. But this person is special. Come what may, I can never say no to him. So I have picked up the pen for the first time in my life to scribble down a story. My shaking fingers are breathing skepticism as I try to gather facts and construct a few meaningful paragraphs. Don't judge me as an author as I am none. My effort would be to take you through the incident with no literary mastery and make you feel close to what I felt years back. The names and characters have been altered here to protect people involved from embarrassment and unnecessary probe into their personal lives.

It was a cold winter evening in Guwahati, Assam when the sun had well set and the mist from the green hills were hurrying down to gather on our rooftops. The lights of the houses in the sparsely populated hills had just started to glow as a jackal howled to welcome the dark. My bungalow was located (it still is since I have been the only constant in the valley for the last sixty years) at the center of the valley so that you could enjoy unhindered beauty of the entire expanse. Thanks to the Municipal Corporation for letting me have the land at a subsidized rate and the low cost of living back then, I had constructed a huge mansion of my dreams decorated with copious stretches of garden both at the front and the back. My back yard had thick foliage of trees as old as Moses as I never touched that part of the land during my house construction. It also had an old well at one desolate corner with a rusted bucket hanging from an even more rusted rod. The water table long gone dry and quenched so many thirsty souls stood ignored and rejected. There was also a brick laden circular path all along the periphery of the garden which came with the well when I acquired the land. Somehow I never touched this garden and let it be the way it was. Someone during his or her prime days must have put a lot of love and affection into this greenery and I never wanted to insult the same. This was where I would take my evening stroll every day completely lost in my thoughts having floated away to a place I never wanted to come back from. That day it was no different. Lost in my reverie as I was crossing the well in the fading light I felt a gush of cold wind hit me on my face. Wondering from where such a sudden cold breeze had started to blow and whether I should go back inside the house now to avoid catching cold, I continued on my path. I had not even moved twenty feet from the well when I felt an eerie feeling behind me. It's like when you know you are being watched from behind and your sixth sense makes you aware of the same. I stopped and slowly turned back.

Let me take a pause here. I know this is the not the right moment in the flow of a story to break it. But it is important for you to know me and my spiritual beliefs before I take you through the next sequence of happenings. Else you won't be able to put your heart and soul into this story.

Born in a staunch Hindu family I grew up in an atmosphere where God in the form of a supernatural power was never questioned but accepted and revered without exception. My dad, who worked as a forest officer here in Assam, was also a deeply religious person and had his shares of encounters with the supernatural all through his life. Many a times he would come back from the jungle and share with me his encounters with ghosts, spirits or the divine. I don't know why but notwithstanding me being the youngest he would share his rich experience with me without hesitation. 'Don't scare the child,' my mom would tell him as he would just smile and choose not to answer. So I grew up accepting this world of shadows as a part of my every day existence. Later as I grew up and carved out my own spiritual world my dad's stories were confirmed through my own experience with the unnatural. Such multiple encounters in my life beyond the realm of human reasoning made me believe without an iota of doubt that we are nothing but souls trapped in this mortal body. Our death marks an event as the soul departs and comes back yet gain in some other form in some other body. The time gap between death and rebirth may vary and that's when they wander hither and thither seeking solace and redemption. I accept them as I accept you, without fear without doubt.

Enough of me, I am sure you must be getting impatient to jump back to the story. So let it be, where was I? Ah! The well, very well....

So there I was hardly having crossed the well as I felt been watched from behind. I slowly turned around. What I saw would have fainted bravest of the brave. But as you know by now my belief and acceptance of the world beyond death had made me intrepid.

There in the well, half lit and half dark floated a lady clad in a typical Bengali white sari with red border looking towards me. Her head was heavily covered in the sari till her temple and hence her face or expression couldn't be made out from where I was standing. She was like a smoke coming out from a house chimney in the winter evening, swaying to communicate something to this world. I did not display any abrupt reaction and slowly started approaching her. I knew if she had come to me she must have come for a reason. I needed to identify her. But the moment I took a few steps towards the well, the smoke dissolved in the background. I hurried to reach the well and called out in an assuring voice, asking her to come back. But all that came back was my own echo from the unknown depth of the well.

I could not sleep well that night. Whenever I would close my eyes the shadowy figure would appear from nowhere and torment me. Who could she be? Why had she come to me? What is it that she wanted to communicate? I wish I had seen her face.

One month went by since that evening as I got busy with my work and almost forgot the incident. A chronic pain in my knee also returned viciously that winter preventing me from taking my evening walks. It was only after the winter was gone I started feeling a bit better and decided to venture out in my garden one evening. All through my walk I never experienced anything on that day even when I went past the well. Maybe she had paid me a visit without any reason, I thought as I ended my walk and was about to walk out of the garden. I don't know why but I felt like giving a last glance at the well and turned around. There she was, standing in her typical signature style waiting to be discovered. This time her head was not covered. But I had come quite a distance from the well. My old eyes could never ever have recognized the face from such a distance. So I slowly started my journey back towards her hoping this time she will not be flying away. As I reached within almost fifteen feet I had a clear vision of her face. The recognition was immediate. She was Kamini, wife of Somnath Sarkar, my ex colleague. She was hale and hearty when I had last met her about three years back. I was invited at her place for dinner on the occasion of my retirement. A very jolly and chirpy girl in her thirties she would so often call me and my wife for dinner. Post my retirement as I had moved away from the office and the people, I had lost touch with everyone and Sarkar was no exception. But what happened to Kamini's beautiful face? Even in the fading twilight I could distinctly see that her entire left side of the face was burnt. Her eyes were full of sorrow as she pleaded for something tacitly. This lasted for a few seconds when she disappeared with me stranded all alone in the garden, poignant.

As the dawn broke after yet another disturbed night of sleep, I knew exactly what to do. Come what may I had to get to the bottom of this and the only way to know the truth was to pay Sarkar a visit. As I reached his house at the other end of the valley and rang the doorbell expecting him to be home on a Sunday morning, the lady who answered the door was not known to me. Well in her twenties she was married.

"Yes?" she asked quizzically.

"I am sorry, but is it Somnath Sarkar's house?" I was hesitant.

"Yes it is. May I know your name?"

"I am Bikash Mitro, he and I used to work together." I responded with some relief having hit upon the right house.

"Oh! Please come in. He has gone to the market but would be back soon." She said politely as she asked me to sit on the sofa in the drawing room.

"Tea?" she asked.

"Well, I would not mind if it's not that inconvenient," I needed a stimulant. The equation was not matching somewhere. Where is Kamini? Who is this lady? Where is their son who if I am not wrong must have been around ten when I had last come here?

As I sat all alone waiting for my cup of tea, I realized nothing had changed in the drawing room. The same sofa where Kamini had sat and chatted till late night, the same wall hangings, the same old grandfather clock ticked away to eternity as I could almost hear her characteristic loud laugh next to me. Something was odd in the air but my sharp sense warned me not to investigate.

"Mitroda? What a pleasant surprise." Sarkar had returned from the market and was standing just inside the door which the lady had kept open.

I smiled and got up from the sofa to shake hands. "Well, I was passing by this place and thought of paying you guys a visit. We have not spoken even once post my retirement."

"Why of course. Please be seated," he said as he took the seat just next to me. The unknown lady entered the room just then and quietly kept down the tea and a plate full of biscuits in front of me. Sarkar was hesitant. I could clearly see his discomfort as he was not sure how to introduce her to me. Judging the situation I smiled at her and said thank you to help her exit the scene quickly. Sarkar's discomfort was growing every minute but I had to get to the bottom of this.

"Where is Kamini?" I made no effort to hide my inquisitiveness.

"She passed away Mitroda, two years back," Sarkar whispered.

"What happened?" I inquired, although Kamini's visit to me had left no room for doubt in my mind that she was no longer in our world.

"It was an unexpected heart attack, middle of the night. I was sleeping right next to her, yet did not realize she was no more!"

He was lying. I could see through him and his flickering eye contact.

"Your son? Where is he?" I was getting impatient.

"I have sent him to a boarding school in North Assam."

"Which one?" I asked.

"Silchor Public School," he replied.

Beyond that I did not have to stay back. I knew exactly what had happened. Kamini must have died two years back when Sarkar brought home his young and attractive second wife. The equation between three of them did not work out when he sent his son to the boarding school. What I had to figure out was what happened to Kamini? Why was Sarkar lying to me? Marrying second time after your spouse is deceased is not a culpable offence. Then why was he so embarrassed and afraid? With all these thoughts hovering over my head I walked out with a deep frown. Sarkar too must have heaved a sigh of relief.

"Modhu, Mitroda this side. Need your urgent help," I had called up ACP Modhusudan Mukherjee to clarify my doubts.

I had known him for the last five years through a common friend and for some reason he had developed a liking for me and respected me like his elder brother.

"Anything for you Mitroda, command."

"I want you to check the records of a death that happened about two years ago here. I can give you the necessary details." I clarified.

"Cake walk, Mitroda. Give me the details and a day. The information will be with you."

True to his words ACP Mukherjee gave me a call exactly after twenty four hours.

"The case is complicated Mitroda. The deceased, Kamini Sarkar suffered ninety degree burn when she was admitted to the hospital. She barely survived through the night. Her husband, Somnath was arrested and put behind bars as a suspect of murder. But interestingly he was let go the very next day and the case was closed. He seems to be having contacts at a very high level. Even more surprising is that no one from the girl's family ever tried to reopen the case." ACP Mukherjee sounded excited.

"Hmm, my suspicion was right. Kamini belonged to a very poor family Modhu and had lost her parents long time back. She hardly had any relatives. So I am not surprised that the case was not touched again."

"Got it. But why are you interested in this particular case?" he was inquisitive.

"Ah? I will tell you sometime later Modhu," I was lost in my thoughts.

"OK. But do let me know if you need any help. I can get the case reopened for you and do a full-fledged investigation if you have any doubts. Culprit or no culprit, we can know the truth and you never know the influence that helped him go scot free back then might no longer exist!"

"Sure Modhu, I will call you if need be. Thanks."

I knew my next steps. The very next day I took a bus to Silchor. I had to meet her estranged son. Fortunately I remembered his first name and asking for him claiming I was his uncle was the easiest part. The toughest part was to control my own emotion when I met him. The ever active, happy go lucky boy whom I met three years back had abruptly matured. Fate, seclusion and misery had made him gallop through his childhood. That smile which had won my heart when I had first handed him a box of chocolate was gone.

"Manik, do you remember me?" I gently asked him touching his shoulder.

A faint nod from him told me he did.

"Manik I know it's difficult for you, but I need to know what exactly happened to your Mom. Believe me it is for her. She has asked me to," I pleaded looking into his eyes.

Children have intelligence beyond the comprehension of us matured individuals. They can see through people much easily than us. He looked straight into my eyes and said, "I don't know Uncle. I was not at home. Dad had asked me to go to one of my friend's house. When I came back they were taking her to the hospital and did not let me see her even once. The gas stove burst is what they said." No tears, no emotion in the voice. The child had turned into a stone.

"And since when you are here dear?" Tears had already started rolling down my cheeks.

"Ever since he married again Uncle, which was within six months of Ma passing away."

I sat down to bring my face close to his and hugged and kissed his head.

"Manik, this will end. I promise you. You have been brave; just hold on for some more time."

With this I breezed out of the school wiping my eyes. The little boy stood there with a perplexed look holding the box of chocolates I had taken for him. He looked at the box wondering what is in it to excite the kids, sighed and walked back to his class.

"Sarkar, Mitro this side." I had called up Somnath the very day I reached back home.

"Yes Mitroda?" I could almost see his frightened face over the phone.

"Kamini never suffered a heart attack. She was burnt to death, ninety degree. Why did you lie to me?" My voice was cold and furious at the same time.

There was almost a thirty seconds silence on the other side before he spoke.

"It was an accident Mitroda. She was in the kitchen when the stove burst. Believe me. I myself suffered burns in my hand trying saving her. You can come and check," he was in tears.

"I don't need to come and check your wounds long healed Sarkar. I don't know what and how it all happened. But all I can tell you what you did to Manik is unacceptable. How could you send him away when he needed you the most?" My irritation and anger was now going beyond my control.

"I could not have Mitroda. My wife and he never got along and there was a continuous unrest in the house."

"Who should be blamed for that? What kind of a father are you to have chosen your wife over your own blood?" I shouted.

There was no answer from the other side. I continued, "Sarkar, you need to get your son back here with you. He cannot stay in a hostel. If you think you are the only person with contacts at the right level then you are wrong. I can get the case reopened and harass you like anything till your last day. Don't try me."

"Mitroda, please don't do this to me. I will be ruined. Believe me I did not kill her." Somnath was now down on his knees.

"Get him back in the next two days. I will call you next Sunday." I ordered and kept down the phone.

A decade has gone by since that threatening call of mine. Manik now stays at my house and goes to the university to come back to me every day. He is studying Civil Engineering and most importantly he has got back his characteristic smile. Somnath Sarkar had no option but to bring his son back in the next three days as instructed. But I knew three of them could not survive healthily under the same roof. Within a month I brought him to my home and that's where he has been staying like my third grandchild with unquestioned love and acceptance.

I don't know whether what I did was right or wrong. Modhu inquired with me many a times about the case and why I had shown interest. He still awaits my answer. Opening the Pandora's Box might or might not have sanctified the truth. But sitting today at the twilight of my own life and seeing Manik's beaming face I know I had made the right choice. What I saw that evening remains with me, not even Manik knows till now.

You, for whom I had to pen this story down, are the only other person privy to it. Now that I have put it down I should share it with Manik. He has a right to know and he will. He should know that how much his Ma loved him to have come back. He should know what I saw in those despondent shadowy eyes that evening was not revenge but a pleading request to a man who only could have acted as a bridge between the two worlds.

Kamini never ever came back. I had hoped she would but she didn't. She must be waiting for me on the other side eager to hold my hand and say for one last time, "Mitroda, *dhonyobad.*" It's not going to be long Kamini...I can almost see the door.

you, for whom I had to put the story down, are the only other
person privy to it. Now that I have put it down, I should share
it with Manik. He has a right to know it all himself. He should
know that how much his Ata loved him to name him back. He
should know what I saw in that desperate pair shadow... was
that evertime was not nothing, but a pleading request to mean
... he only could have acted as a bridge between the two worlds.
Kamini never ever came back and hoped she would but
she didn't. She must be somewhere in the otherside again.
I hold my hand out .... turned, and might
It's not going to .... and there, at the door,

12

Alchemist

The sound reverberated across the shop, as Aatmaram Aggarwal slapped Chotu in front of all the employees on a Monday morning, minutes after the shutters opened.

"Do I pay you for sleeping here, you street urchin?" he barked. "Why so much dust on my table?"

"Sorry *Sethji*, I forgot. It won't happen again." He apologized, right ear and cheek red, in painful embarrassment as he started dusting the table with a quiet sob. Not a single employee in the shop dared to protest or come to the rescue of the small boy. A quick cursory glance towards Chotu was the only mark of sympathy they showed.

Aatmaram Aggarwal or more commonly known as Sethji, was a third generation Marwari businessman running a jewelry shop in Chandni Chowk, Old Delhi. Always clad in his white kurta and dhoti with a cap to cover the receding hairline, an abrupt curtain of silence would befall the shop whenever he walked in. Every employee cringed under an eternal threat of being fired at the drop of a hat. Extremely bad tempered and cantankerous, Sethji breathed a miasma to intoxicate the entire shop all day. Yet his employees had no choice but to continue working for him. The market was tough after the global meltdown. People were losing their jobs every day.

So that day when they saw him physically abuse the small boy, no one had the courage to even stare at the scene for a while. They had to choose between job security and humanity, they chose the first.

Our victim, the hapless boy who ran errands in the shop was yet another nameless face in the crowd representing the incompetence of our country to eradicate child labor even today. Ever smiling in spite of the hardship, he looked to be in his early teens as both his actual date of birth and name had been long inundated and extinguished by poverty.

"Does it hurt a lot?" inquired Rashid while applying some ice on Chotu's face, outside the shop during lunchtime.

The red mark of the ring studded fat fingers of Sethji was still evident on his face when he replied with a sad smile, "I am fine Rashid Chacha. This is the price I have to pay all my life for being illiterate, I know that. Life has taught me to accept humiliation with a glee."

The words in the form a desolate sarcasm caused turmoil in Rashid's soft heart. He felt like rushing back to the shop and giving it back to the obnoxious owner then and there. He felt like rescuing this boy from this drudgery and giving him a better life. But he could do none. With his hands tied by the gnarled rope of circumstances, he was no exception. A helpless glance exchanged, submerged in dreadful silence of acceptance, both went back to work.

Rashid Khan was a wonderful craftsman when it came to making gold jewelry. Having assisted his Abba since childhood, he had mastered his skills quite young. His Abba also worked for the same jewelry shop for the past twenty years. So when he died a sudden death six months back, it was but obvious that Rashid would step into his shoes. So in he came, having to abruptly abandon his studies, sit in one corner of the shop to bend and work all day melting and shaping human desire. He soon realized that along with the hard work his Abba had also left him the frugal salary as part of the deal. He was astonished to realize that his Abba had been working at half the salary that he should have got. Frustrated he decided to approach Sethji one day.

"*Hazoor*, I had one request to make," Rashid had walked up to Sethji's desk at the other end of the shop.

"Yes, what is it?" replied an ever irritated Aatmaram.

"Hazoor, I am sorry to say but I think you are underpaying me. Same job and experience in the market would fetch at least double of what you are paying me," Rashid blurted out.

Sethji was livid as he looked at Rashid. "Underpaid is it? Your dad worked with me for twenty years and never ever did he come up asking for a raise. He was happy and content with whatever I would pay him and look at you! Not even six months in the job and you have the audacity to walk up to me asking for a salary revision? I should be actually paying you less than what I paid your dad going by your experience!"

"Hazoor, with due respect to you and my Abba, judge my quality of work not by the number of years I have put in. None of your customers have any complaint, in fact the modern style I have brought in has increased your clientele."

"Phooh! And so you think you are worth more is it? Why don't you leave this job and go where they pay you double? Go and give it a shot. Come back to me once you have had a reality check. The problem with this young generation is greed. You are never satisfied with what you have and always desire for more."

Rashid understood that there was no point arguing with this person any further and went back to work, sulking.

The economic meltdown had shifted faith to the old and trusted as people started investing more and more in gold ornaments, coins and bonds. Aatmaram Aggarwal was euphoric as his business started to flourish beyond expectation. He was planning to expand his shop by incorporating the adjacent sweet shop. All he needed was one good deal.

When the white ambassador with a red VIP light flashing and stamped 'On Government Duty' escorted by two Honda City came and stopped in front of his shop on a Monday afternoon, he thought that some high official from the income tax department must have come for a raid. With so much of black money floating everywhere, it was a common site in Chandni Chowk gold market. But when he saw the official getting down from the car along with a lady who looked to be his wife and two children approaching his shop, he was flustered. He knew it was his lucky day and shouted at the top of his voice, "Alert everyone, put your best foot forward, we have a VIP in our shop."

Before the VIP could enter the shop, his two hugely built body guards clad in black body hugging attire, entered and without talking to anyone started checking every nook and corner of the shop and eyeing every employee. Satisfied, they then walked up to Aatmaram who was sitting on his *gadda* with a sheepish smile.

"You are the owner?" one of the bodyguards inquired.

"Ye...yess," Aatmaram was stammering out of fear and excitement.

"OK, we have our boss here who is flying to London for a Worldwide Conference. He had a stopover here in Delhi and wanted to shop for his wife. She wants to pick up some very expensive gold set which can be worn during the conference when she is there in London. Do you think you would have something good?" The Black Cat was fluent.

Aatmaram's eyes immediately lighted up. "Why of course. Please ask them to come in."

What followed in the next one hour was a complete pandemonium in the shop. Everyone including Sethji himself was at the display counter exhibiting the most expensive and heavy gold jewelry sets to the lady. Her husband kept on looking impatiently at his watch while their kids sat with a bored expression at one corner of the shop. Some customers left with utter disgust after having received no attention from the sales girls. Mrs. VIP to Sethji's dismay turned out to be a very fastidious shopper. Whatever was shown to her she would reject with a frown on her face. After more than an hour of this Mr. VIP got up from his seat irate and irritated and called for his wife, "Sonia, we are getting late. We have the flight to catch; I don't have the whole day. If you think this shop is not good enough, let's go to some other one, there are plenty on this street."

"Sir, please be patient. Chotu, go get some chocolates for the kids and cold drink for saab, hurry. Sir you sit, I do have something which Her Highness will like. I generally don't display it." As Chotu ran like a whirlwind to fetch the things from the adjacent shop, Aatmaram hurriedly bent down to take out a huge velvet box from his vault. The dazzling piece of art in the box would have impressed Noor Jahan had she made a time travel to future. It was a complete set of necklace, ear rings and bangles all made of pure gold studded with diamonds all over. The entire set must have weighed close to one kilogram or so, enough to cause cervical rupture even before paying for it. But female anatomy since ages has demonstrated a unique behavioral pattern when it comes to gold. Their apparently fragile bones miraculously turn tough when it comes to carrying gold ornaments. Mrs. VIP was no exception. As she stood in front of the full scale mirror with the entire set on her, Sethji knew for sure that the deal was cracked. Rashid looked back over his shoulder and smiled. It was his best work of art till date. He had taken two arduous months to complete this masterpiece. He felt satisfied that his talent was being appreciated.

"How much for this?" asked the VIP having read his wife's thought.

"Sir, this is the most expensive piece I have in the shop. You can see the intricate craftsmanship and the amount of gold and diamonds that have gone in to give it this luster," bragged Aatmaram.

"I know, I know. Don't waste my time, get to the point," he had a flight to catch.

"It's two and a half crores Sir, I will give a ten percent discount on the same, just for you."

"Hmm, look, I hate haggling, not my cup of tea. Give me twenty five percent and I will take it right now."

"Sir, it's too much for me. I would be selling at a loss," pleaded Aatmaram.

"Oh come on, don't give me all that bull shit. I am really getting late. Take it or leave it," Mr. VIP had started walking towards the door. The kids jumped to follow hoping the ordeal had finally ended while Mrs. VIP still stood in front of the mirror basking in the glory of the necklace.

"Sir, please, don't get angry. Here have a seat. OK, I will give it to you at twenty percent discount and please don't push me further. I am only doing it for you as you are an honored guest and I don't want you to go away from my shop disappointed."

"OK, then get it packed," barked Mr. VIP as he took out his check book. "Against whose name should I write the check?" he inquired.

"Sir, check? Can't you pay in cash or card?" Aatmaram was skeptical.

"What's the problem? Who on earth carries so much of cash? You want me to go shopping with a suitcase full of cash, is it? And by the way I being of the old school, never carry a credit card," Mr. VIP was furious.

"Sir, debit card...," whispered Sethji.

"This is ridiculous. Guys let's move out of this shop. You do one thing, here is my visiting card. Please call up the bank and enquire the authenticity of my identity and also check the amount I have in the account. By then I would be flying over the middle east," mocked Mr. VIP as he threw his visiting card on Sethji's face. His two ominous body guards by then had taken positions on both sides of their boss and stared down Sethji's throat.

"OK, OK, Sir. Please don't be so angry. You know how this world has become. You have to be extra careful. Please draw a check in the name of the shop," Sethji was perspiring by then.

As the executive entourage left, everyone in the shop heaved a sigh of relief. Sethji took off his cap, wiped his sweat and relaxed on his gaddi with arms stretched.

"Chotu, put the fan on full speed and get me a Thumbs up, hurry," he shouted as he looked at the check of two crores staring at him with a beaming face. It was of the same bank he had his account. He glanced at his watch and realized that if he dashed to the nearest branch and deposited the check, the money would get credited first thing in the morning tomorrow. All his lethargy was gone in an instant as he jumped out of his seat, adjusted his cap and ran past Chotu snatching the Thumbs Up bottle from his hand, pushing him from the way and almost making him fall.

That night Aatmaram Aggarwal had a sound sleep as he dreamt himself walking into his new expanded shop showcasing double the pomp and glory. As he woke up in the morning the very first thing he did was check his mobile for any update from his bank. None.... He looked at the watch; it was five in the morning. It's a little too early for the bank to deal with transactions, he thought. Since then he kept on checking his mobile every fifteen minutes with no results. It was well past mid-day and he had started to get worried. Unable to handle the tension that was building up inside him, he decided to pay a visit to the nearest branch where he had deposited the check yesterday.

"Yes Sir, how can I help you?" asked the professionally clad young lady at the customer care.

"Ma'am, I had deposited this check yesterday afternoon. It belongs to this bank only and hence my expectation was that it should have got credited by now. But I have not received any update in my mobile. Can you please check?"

"Sure, please take a seat Sir."

As she looked at the Xerox of the check Sethji had handed over to her and started checking the details in the computer, she became serious and the expression on her face changed within seconds.

"Sir, can you please accompany me to the Manager's cabin," she requested.

Sethji got up and followed her anxiously till the cabin as she knocked on the door.

"Sir, he has come," she indicated to the Manager as if something had already been discussed.

"Sir please come in, have a seat," requested the Manager to Sethji.

"May I ask you who gave you this check Mr. Aggarwal?"

"Why has it bounced?" Aatmaramhad already started feeling flutters in his stomach.

"Bounced? Haha. Mr. Aggarwal, this account does not even exist with us, it never did. There is no person with this name of Ajay Tiwari in our data base. This is a forged check book duplicated so well that even we missed it at the first glance. I am sorry Sir. Whoever it was has pulled up a great one on you. I hope you have not sold something based on the check?"

There was pin drop silence in the room as Aatmaram could not believe what the manger was telling him. He still thought it was all a joke and would pass. He felt someone was banging on his chest with a hammer only to realize it was his own heartbeat.

"Now...?" All that came out of his choked voice was a whimper.

"Well Sir, if you ask me, the first thing you should do is to go to the police station and file a report."

"How could you sell such a costly thing basis a check?" shouted the incredulous young police officer after having listened to the whole story from Aatmaram.

"Sir, it was so much real. His government car with a siren, his bodyguards, his family, his demeanor, the check book, everything. There was no way anyone could have doubted his credibility, Sir, in that hour." justified Sethji.

"Phooh! Grow up Sethji. Do you know how little it takes to get those things organized? I am sure you never bothered to note down the car registration number. Even if you had, believe me those false plates would be now lying in some remote gutter waiting to be sold as scrap metal by an urchin. You know what is your problem Sethji? It's your greed."

"What now Sirjee? Would he be caught?" Aatmaram was in tears. His insatiable avarice has slapped him on his face."

"File a report. We will try and see. I will come to your shop tomorrow. But don't pin much hope on this Sethji. Consider the necklace set gone to charity."

One month passed with Sethji regularly making a visit to the police station enquiring the progress. The VIP conman along with his imposter entourage had vanished in thin air. Aatmaram Aggarwal was heartbroken. His shop continued to be of the same size as he gloomily observed his rival businessman buy the adjacent shop.

"Khan Chacha, Khan Chacha, something unbelievable has happened," Chotu had come running to Rashid's house early in the morning.

"Yes Chotu, what is it?"

"Yesterday someone contacted my mother saying they would take the entire responsibility of my education! They called themselves some NGO, I don't know what that means. It seems some unidentified person contacted them and made this specific demand. I can't understand Chacha, who could it be? No one that I know of would spend even ten rupees on me."

Rashid's mind floated back in time. Instigated by insatiable hatred for his employer and sympathy for the little boy, he could not but take this calculated risk. A meticulous planning clubbed with enticing the right resources with the potential reward finally did the trick. He had to forego the lion's share, but he had no regrets. All he wanted was an amount that could see through the child's education and a decent upbringing. The look on sethji's face had more than compensated his share.

"Chacha, Chacha, what are you thinking? Did you hear what I just said?" Chotu was impatient.

"Yes I did. Why are you worried about who the person is, Chotu? Tell me one thing, are you happy?" Rashid had jumped back to present.

"Happy? Chacha I am on the ninth cloud. You know it was my dream to get educated and break the shackle of bondage. This is like a dream. I wish I knew who that messiah was!"

Rashid had tears in his eyes as he lifted Chotu in his arms and kissed him.

Melting and shaping gold to quench human desire, Rashid had become an anonymous Alchemist in Chotu's dreams forever.

✦ ✦ ✦

13

Remedy

As Shyam entered his bedroom hearing an unnatural sound, the view in front of his eyes petrified him. It was as if the most bizarre scene from a horror film had been picked up and enacted in his room. Bandana, his wife for the past five years, was lying on the floor, writhing in pain. She was having severe convulsions and was frothing from her mouth as her terror stricken eyes searched for help. Shyam's initial thought was that she must be having her regular feats of epileptic seizures again. But as he hurriedly went near, he realized that Bandana was in a unique state of morbidity which defied all logic. She had her left hand on her own neck trying with all her might to strangle herself. While her right hand tried in frantic desperation to free the left hand to save her! It was as if the demon and angel deep within her had suddenly appeared in person to have conflict in the open.

"Bandana, what's wrong? What are you doing? Why are you choking yourself?" Shyam shouted in alarm as he rushed to the floor to assist her. But all he could hear was a faint cry of help from his wife, a desperate effort to communicate to her husband through her strangulated vocal cord. The grip of the demon hand was so strong that even Shyam could not untangle it. It was as if Bandana had conjured up herculean strength from nowhere. Shyam remembered their house physician having told him once, at the time of acute epilepsy sometimes a counter shock helped revive the patient. Not having any other option with him, he lifted Bandana, made her somehow stand and slapped her with all his strength. The brutal force threw her off feet as she went flying to land on the bed and blacked out. Shyam then slowly untangled the demon and the angel to make them rest peacefully next to her, while covering her with a sheet.

It was a cold winter night in Kolkata, a few days before Christmas. Yet he was perspiring heavily. He was still to come out of the shock and sat next to the bed for a few minutes to gather himself. His hands and legs were shaking still as he picked up the mobile and called up Dr. Sarkar, their long-time family physician and friend.

"Doc, Shyam this side."

"Yes, Shyam, all well? You sound terrible!"

"Can you come down immediately? Something terrible has happened to Bandana," exclaimed Shyam.

"Is it the seizure once again?" inquired the doctor.

"It was, but this time it was a bizarre one. I can't explain over the phone, you need to come and see her."

"Is she out of it now?"

"Yes, she is sleeping."

"Ok then, I am leaving my chamber in the next fifteen minutes. I should be at your place by 9. Don't worry, just stay next to her."

Shyam disconnected the phone and decided to cool himself with a can of chilled beer as he waited for the doctor's arrival. Bandana was sleeping peacefully. As if she had very efficiently cut herself off the past few traumatic minutes of her life and taken refuge in a simpler world. Shyam held her hand and looked on as he drifted into the past....

He still remembered the first time he saw Bandana at her father's place five years back. Short and fair, as she entered the room with a hint of shyness and reluctance on her face, Shyam was instantly smitten. He had gone along with his Mom to meet Bandana and her parents as part of their routine search for a suitable bride. Shyam had been working for a multinational company for the past five years and had decided to settle down. However, being extremely shy in nature he had no other option but to seek his mom's help in this matter. Bandana belonged to an educated middle class family and had just completed M.A. in Bengali. Both the families liked each other on the very day. The two would-be husband and wife were also allowed some time in private in an adjacent room, where they developed a liking through a short and tacit conversation. The horoscopes shook hands in agreement. The most auspicious day was calculated in the coming winter, barely one month from that day. Shyam's mom was a bit hesitant due to such a short notice, but Bandana's parents emphasized on the holiness of the day and got her to agree. Before the blink of an eye, they were married. Shyam stepped into his new life ecstatic and optimistic – all ready to start a memorable life with his strikingly beautiful wife.

Least did he know he was building a house of cards.

Within six months of their marriage, he realized that the haste shown by her family to perform the marriage at the first available day had nothing to do with the holiness of the hour. Apparently flawless, Bandana was chronically epileptic. Her family having failed to marry her off for quite a while due to this stigma of hers had planned to hide it this time. Trustworthy and gullible, Shyam and his mom were the unfortunate victims. His mom was furious to start with and took out all her wrath and malice on Bandana and her parents. Shyam was also irate. More than that, he was hurt and had felt sad and cheated. He never reprimanded Bandana for this though. He had just asked her once, "How did you or your Dad ever think a lifelong relationship could be built on lack of transparency and trust?"

Bandana had no answer to that. She had wanted to share this, like she had done on all other occasions when the bridal families backed out. But this time she was specifically asked to keep quiet. Reluctantly, she had obeyed. Possibly she had thought that this was her last chance. Maybe she believed somehow she would make things work once married. Maybe she thought the holy thread of marriage would give her a miraculous cure. No one knew and she never shared. But Shyam's dream of building Utopia was scorched even by the first rays of the sun. His mom asked him to file a divorce. He even contemplated once. But as he looked into those despondent eyes of Bandana sitting rejected in one corner of the house, his heart overflowed with sympathy. He knew this was a medical condition, beyond her control. He at times, put himself in her shoes and enacted the scenes to realize that having been discarded by the society for a flaw well beyond human control maybe he too would have taken a chance. He also felt responsible for her future imagining what would happen to her if he divorced her on medical grounds. And so, Shyam Sanyal, a compassionate honest man and a staunch believer in destiny, accepted Bandana as his formally wedded wife, just like the diamond studded night sky accepts the scar faced elegant moon as its own.

The doorbell rang. Shyam looked at his watch. It was fifteen minutes past nine. It must be Dr. Sarkar, he thought.

"How is she?" asked Dr. Sarkar worried as he entered.

"Still sleeping."

"Hmm, let me check."

After he completed his routine check on Bandana, she continued to sleep. He then came out to the drawing room and sat on the sofa.

"Her BP is normal. She has no fever or stiffness in her muscles. She seems pretty okay. Now tell me, what exactly happened to have psyched you like this?"

As Shyam narrated the entire incident meticulously, not leaving out any detail, the doctor listened with rapt attention.

"Hmm...have you ever observed this trait in her when she went into her fits?" asked the doctor, his frown on his forehead multiplying every second.

"No, never.... She would have her seizures once every six months. You are well aware of that. But nothing close to what happened today."

"Hmmm...okay, Shyam. I have given her an injection. She would be sleeping like a log till late morning tomorrow. Take it easy. Talk to her tomorrow once she is okay and do let me know."

"Thanks Doc, I know it's quite late."

Next day morning as Bandana woke up, she was still dizzy. As she dragged her slightly disoriented self to the dining table, Shyam came out of the kitchen, kissed her on the head and asked, "Tea?"

"Yes, please," she replied softly.

As he put the kettle on the gas oven he asked in a matter of fact way from the kitchen, "How are you feeling?"

"Much better Shyam, much better...that intense dark cloud of depression is no longer looming on my head. I am feeling much lighter."

"Do you recall what happened? Was it your usual cycle of depression followed by the seizure?" inquired Shyam gently.

"This time it was different Shyam and that's why I also got scared out of my wits. I had no control over my left hand as it went for my neck. I had an inexorable urge to kill myself. I realized at the same time that I should not be doing it and hence tried to save myself using my right hand. But the left hand had so much power!!!" Bandana was still getting shivers from the thought.

"Now, don't get worked up. Dr. Sarkar was here last night. He checked you and said everything is normal. Let's not think about last evening. I hope you are continuing with the antidepressants on a regular basis?"

As she gently nodded, Shyam gently hugged her. In the last five years of marriage, Shyam had grown to love Bandana deeply in spite of the jumpy start. Barring the occasional medical malfunction, Bandana was a perfect wife. She also reciprocated his love with interest, as she had the element of respect and gratitude in her. She knew in her heart that no one else would have accepted her the way Shyam had. She considered herself lucky.

Their relationship was going well. The void created at times by the absence of kids was made up with their ever burning passion for each other. However, in the last one year, Shyam observed that Bandana would get into a state of depression for no apparent reason and would stay like that for two to three days. Then a typical trend started to develop. After each cycle of depression she would have the seizure. Yesterday evening it was expected, as she had been in her low for the past few days. That is why he came from office early, pre-empting. But what happened with her was beyond his wildest dream.

He just hoped that this was a one off incident and that she would be fine.

The attack recurred after two weeks and this time it struck with a vengeance. By the time Shyam discovered, she had lost her consciousness and was hardly breathing. She had to be hospitalized for two days. After that, life never went back to normal for Shyam and Bandana. Both of them equally dreaded the onset of the attack. With every passing month it grew in frequency and became increasingly random and unpredictable. They went to multiple Neuro specialists in Kolkata, but no one could decipher the reason behind this weird self-destructive behavior. All they would prescribe was sleeping pills and nerve relaxants which had no effect. Shyam now could hardly go out leaving her alone, as both of them were equally afraid of that dark hour.

Dr. Sarkar called up one day, "Shyam, good news. There is a worldwide seminar on neuroscience that's happening this weekend and its happening here in Kolkata. All top Neuro specialists from across the world would be coming here. I am sure we will have our answer amongst them. I have already sent across the case study to them. They will discuss amongst themselves and will let us know. So let's hope for the best."

Bandana's case became a subject of long discussion and argument amongst the stalwarts who had gathered to deliver their own lectures. None of them had heard of this kind of a behavior before. Each one of them built their own theory and no conclusion could be arrived rest aside any cure. They would study Bandana as model bombarding her with myriad questions, making her feel even more uncomfortable, conscious and depressed. After two days of this relentless drama, Shyam got fed up and stopped taking Bandana to them.

It was on the third day when he received a call. It was a British accent as someone spoke from the other side, "Shyam Sanyal? I am Dr. Thomas Davy. We are sorry to have put you through this. But can we meet today for the last time? It would be just me I promise."

Reluctant, yet hopeful, Shyam and Bandana reached the hotel room as Dr. Davy had instructed.

"Please be comfortable Ma'am. Mr. Sanyal, please have a seat," a very cordial Dr. Davy showed them the sofa in his hotel room.

He was an old man, with white hair, beard and moustache covering his entire face. He seemed to have jumped out of Harry Potter's characters rather than being a Neuro Specialist, Shyam thought.

"Let me again apologize for what you had to go through, Ma'am. Your case is so typical that we had to storm our brains to get to the root of it and hence you experienced that pandemonium. We still have divided opinions amongst us, but I wanted to share with you what I and some of my very senior colleagues think is the cause of your behavior.

"Now before I tell you that let me enlighten you about the human brain – at about 1.4 kg in weight, it is the most complicated organ we have in our body. It is so complex that our knowledge of it today is equivalent to man's knowledge of the universe when we first accepted that the Earth circles the sun. Now to understand why this is happening, you need to understand few basic functions of the brain.

"The human brain is divided into two hemispheres, the left and right, connected by a structure called the corpus callosum. The hemispheres are strongly, though not entirely, symmetrical. The left brain controls all the muscles on the right-hand side of the body; and the right brain controls the left side. One hemisphere may be slightly dominant, as with left or right-handedness.

"The left brain is associated with mathematical calculation and fact retrieval. The right brain plays a role in visual and auditory processing, spatial skills and artistic ability. In simple words Mrs. Sanyal, our left half is for logic and the right half is for emotion. The corpus callosum is like an elastic band which connects these two hemispheres and maintains a balance between our logical and emotional self. If for some reason this balance gets disrupted, one half would dominate over the other. Are you with me till now?"

A faint nod from the intrigued Sanyals gave Dr. Davy the consent to carry on.

"Good. Now comes the most interesting part. Since when have you been having your epileptic seizures Ma'am?"

"Since I was six, I think," replied Bandana.

"Hmm...it seems that the repeated attacks very slowly damaged your corpus callosum. Now as I understand from having interacted with you in the last few days, you have always had these cycles of depression that you would get into time and again since childhood. Now, till the time your corpus callosum was functioning fine, your logical brain rationalized with your emotional brain and ironed it out. But as your corpus callosum got damaged your cycles of depression also started getting elongated and finally when the damage was significant, your emotional half completely took over the charge. Hence when you got depressed and felt like ending this life, your left side of the brain had no way of communicating back to its counterpart that we should be optimistic about life and give it one more chance. Now if you remember, the left brain controls all the muscles on the right-hand side of the body; and the right brain controls the left side. So when you get this attack of depression, your right brain commands your left hand to kill yourself and end this malady. Thus guided by reflex it tries to strangle you.

"This is the most interesting and one of its kind case of brain anomaly that I have come across in my fifty years of professional career, I must admit." Accepted the doctor.

Both Shyam and Bandana were stupefied. Bandana did not know how to react. Whether to be happy knowing from this foreign doctor that she was one in a million in this entire world or be sad that she could not be an average woman leading an insignificant life?

"Remedy Doctor?" asked Shyam with half hope and half despair.

"Well, Mr. Sanyal, I will be very honest with you here. The only logical solution seems to be replacing the corpus callosum which going by today's medical capability is not feasible. So the only feasible solution is training your own brain through yoga and meditation. You have to learn to control your logical left side Mrs. Sanyal so as to consciously dominate your emotional right. The reason why I told you everything in such detail is because many a times, knowing the actual problem helps in solving rationalizing the brain functions.

"So my suggestion to both of you would be, don't lose hope. At least you have a known devil to tackle. Be positive and fight the battle together. You are a brave young lady Mrs. Sanyal, full of vigor and vitality. You have displayed so much of courage till now, I am sure you will win. All the best. Here is my visiting card, feel free to drop me a mail or call me if you need any help."

The next six months went by with Bandana and Shyam trying to accept their fate and also making an effort to divert its course. Shyam took her to a renowned yoga guru who gave her a few yogas to practice every day and also helped her with a few tips on meditation. Be it for the yoga or the fact that they now knew the cause, the frequency of the attacks went down. However, at least once a month it would come back like an unannounced tornado, demolishing everything in its way. Every time as it went away, it would leave both of them physically and emotionally drained. It was no remedy. It was just delaying the inevitable.

That year, West Bengal experienced the highest rainfall in history. The coastal area in Orissa suffered a severe depression shoulder to shoulder with Bandana and cried uncontrollably. The spillover affected the adjacent state to bring havoc and devastation across. Kolkata, well known for its incompetent drainage system was completely waterlogged. The carnage of strong wind, rain and thunder continued relentlessly.

Bandana had again gone into her black hole. Shyam knew that the attack was coming any moment. An ayurvedic doctor had given Bandana a medicine which to Bandana's belief was helping her. She had developed a trust in that drug. But she had run out of stock and desperately wanted it hoping that it would prevent the attack. The shop was about five kilometers away and would take Shyam at least thirty minutes if not more in this heavy rain to go and get the drug. Now, he never wanted to leave Bandana alone in this state, but Bandana was insistent on the medicine. With no option left, he decided to take Bandana along. He knew a short cut through which his scooter would go. Both covered in raincoats, they leaped on their two wheeler and headed towards the pharmacy.

They could never reach their destination.

The storm had uprooted an electric pole on the way which having fallen on the flooded ground had electrocuted an entire by lane that Shyam had decided to take. They were thrown off the scooter like Barbie dolls. It was a complete blackout.

The earth had taken a complete round around the sun since that dreadful day. Either due to delayed assistance on the tempestuous evening or the extremely high degree of voltage generated from the broken down transformer pole, Shyam could not survive. Bandana was unconscious in the hospital for an entire day, but miraculously survived. It took her a long time to get out of the shock. It was months before she spoke to anyone. The monsoon had left, the rains had dried, the flooded streets had become innocuous mud puddles, but Bandana's soul had the thunder, lightning and rain trapped inside, forever.

But one interesting change came over her. In spite of this infinite void and despair, she never had those suicidal attacks again. It was as if the reflection of her life in the mirror had flipped positions. With Shyam next to her and all the reasons to be elated, she had relentlessly tried to destroy herself. Now with him gone from her life forever having all the reasons to end her futile existence, she could do it no more.

Intense and electrifying despair had turned her demon hand euphoric....

✦ ✦ ✦

14

Kailash

"Sons, you can consider this as my last wish. It doesn't necessarily mean you have to fulfill it. All dreams in our life are not meant to be touched by reality."

"What is it Ma?"

"I want to do Kailash Yatra."

"Kailash as in Mt. Kailash in Tibet?"

"Yes, the holy abode of Lord Shiva and the heavenly Mansarovar Lake."

"Ma, are you out of your mind? Do you even realize what you are wishing for? The lake is at an altitude of close to 20,000 ft. above sea level. The overall journey stretches through twenty days in one of the harshest terrain ever known to mankind. Even young people hesitate to dare and you at this age want to make that arduous journey? Why do you want to call for such hardship on you?"

"I told you, it's my wish. Doesn't mean you have to take it seriously. I have lived my life with myriad dreams dreamt in vain, million wishes wished in pain; let this be yet another one. Let me complete my sons, I need your patient listening tonight."

"OK Ma, go ahead, we are listening."

"My wish is that all three of you make this yatra with me. Even if one of you drops of, I don't want to go to Lord Shiva. All or none is the only condition I have."

Her three sons were dumbfounded as they looked at each other not able to answer anything in reply. Judging their reaction she said, "You don't have to answer me right now. Talk amongst yourself and let me know. There is no emotional pressure from my side and I am not dying tomorrow. I know the trip is not only long but expensive too. All of you are busy with your work and hardly have any time for yourselves or your families. The least I can do is contribute my own share. I have some money left by your dad. So take your time and think through. Whatever is your decision don't hesitate coming back to me and sharing the same. Remember, I have seen too much in life to be hurt anymore."

As her three sons walked out draped in pregnant silence, she gathered herself on the bed and opened her small aluminum box to make her betel leaf. This was the only weakness Giribala Devi still fought to overcome, her addiction to paan. Standing at the crossroad of life and beyond she had been able to detach herself mentally from almost all facets of life. But this last hitch and yet another desire to visit the heavenly abode, remained like a straw still binding her to this materialistic world. She wanted to break free, she had seen too much.

Ten years back when she unexpectedly lost her husband, she was left in a state of shock and three sons Abhiroop, Abhishek and Abhigyan to deal with. No, she never had to struggle for either money or their education. Fortunately her husband, Suryoprakash, had earned enough to have left her with no worries for the rest of her life. The three sons also were all well established by then and never needed any financial support from their mom. All three of them were extremely close to Giribala as compared to their father who always had maintained a formal distance with his sons. So when she became alone all three of them got even more caring about their mom and saw to it that she had no degree of discomfort in any aspect of life. Anybody and everybody who knew them and her would quote it as an epitome of good fostering by Giribala. It's all due to the Almighty, she would say. But deep within her knew how much of sacrifice she had to make to see a day like this, what an onerous path she had to traverse day and night with her husband staying aloof all along, to arrive at this rosy destination. Having grown up and seen the cold and selfish relationship amongst her own five brothers the last thing she wanted was to see a reflection of the same in her own sons. She wanted them to grow as one team bonded together with love, peace and mutual respect. She ensured zero discrimination and uncontrolled shower of love and values to all three. She even went to the extent of sheltering them from any influence whatsoever of their uncles by reducing her own trips to her mom's place. Yes, she did succeed. They grew up most definitely as a team and could take the entire world together. This went along for a significant period of time till they were all established, to give Giribala Devi a sense of achievement and satisfaction. Alas, to her dismay her castle was blown away by a hurricane after Suryoprakash died.

Suryoprakash having earned a lot his entire life had built two mansions, both in the heart of South Kolkata. Although it never took him a fortune to build it years back, thanks to the sky rocketing real estate prices, by the time he died both these mansions were sitting on millions. One of them was where they stayed as they rented out the other. Unexpected death never gave Suryoprakash time to draft a will. To make matters worse he had both the properties in his own name. Abhiroop, Abhishek and Abhigyan never wanted to disturb the peace of their mom and hence had a unified decision of not touching the ancestral house where she stayed. It was the other house which stirred the hornet's nest. Abhiroop, the eldest and elder to Abhishek by five years and Abhigyan by eleven wanted to sell it off. The business he was in was not doing well for the past few years. He was cash strung and had debt in the market. He saw this opportunity to bail out quickly and efficiently. Abhishek, the middle one, working for a multinational firm as a civil engineer and not in need of immediate money, wanted to take it easy. He wanted to demolish the mansion and construct a skyscraper to then sell off at high profit margin. He knew that if handed over to a promoter the lion's share of the profit would most definitely be taken away. He never wanted to let go that. Abhigyan, the youngest working as a Chartered Accountant in an established foreign multinational never wanted this house to be demolished. He knew that the bricks and mortars had their father's sweat imprinted on them. He never wanted to annihilate the emotional bond. He also knew if the house was brought to the ground, their mom would be hurt. She might or might not express the same as she was an extremely strong woman. But deep within he knew she would encounter a devastating jolt.

Thus, stood the team nurtured with love and trained to agree, loggerheads with each other with three disparate opinions on the future of the house. Mild disagreements to start with the discussions soon started ending in bitter quarrels. The golden yardstick was now being used to test the purity of bond and they were failing. Giribala Devi alarmed by the imminent danger called multiple meetings with her three sons to bring them on the same page. But to her sheer despair, she realized each time they would hit the cul-de-sac. Days turned to months to years as no needle movement happened towards taking a decision. The only significant and visible change appeared in the relationship of the three brothers. They were no longer a team. They were just three team members who hardly spoke to each other having no common motif of survival. The only common thread knitting them together was Giribala Devi herself. Desiring desperately she dreaded to die. She knew the moment she would be gone her three sons would move apart like the myriad galaxies after the Big Bang never to meet again.

"Does she even know what is she talking?" Abhiroop was evidently irate and was talking to his two younger brothers in an animated way. "I am not even sure whether she would be allowed at her age. The last I knew the maximum age limit was seventy. How old is she Abhigyan?"

"She will be sixty nine this year *Dada*," replied Abhigyan promptly.

"Still, what about the medical tests? I have heard the Ministry is very strict with the tests and those need to be conducted from a few selected hospitals in Delhi only. Then you have the hassles of getting a Chinese visa too to enter Tibet not to talk of the extreme hardship for the three weeks' time period. If you listen to me this is sheer lunacy. I think senility has started to settle in her," Abhiroop declared.

"Don't forget the cost part. Last year a friend of mine had gone and he spent more than a lakh just for himself. Even if Ma bears her own expense, I am not in a situation to shell out a lakh right now." Abhishek announced.

"Neither am I," shouted Abhiroop.

Abhigyan, the youngest was sitting quietly in one corner not having spoken a single word till then.

"Gyan, what is your view? Don't just sit like that in the corner," Abhishek addressed the youngest.

"All I want to say here is don't be so judgmental on Ma. I know her wish is not the easiest to be fulfilled but she has not wished for the moon either! I am sure there would be an easier way out. With tourism being promoted so much now there has to be travel agencies taking care of all the hassles. Why don't we find out and then decide?" he requested.

"It would have been easier if she had wished for the moon Gyan, much easier. At least we could have explained the absurdity of the thought and said no. What about the finance? Who is going to arrange for that? If you would have agreed to get rid of that sentimental mansion we all would have been able to pull this off at ease. You were the one who never wanted to hurt Ma's sentiments, right? Now you only decide which sentiment you want to protect and how!" Abhishek was furious.

"Mejda, please, don't start it all over again and you know it was just not me holding back a final decision. Anyway, let me get back to you on the travel logistics. We will talk on the finance later," Abhigyan delivered his speech looking out of the window and then walked out of the room with a heavy sigh.

"There are two ways of reaching Kailash," Abhigyan had regathered with his brothers within a week with all the necessary information. "The first one is by air as in by the helicopter and the other one by road. The aerial route will take ten to twelve days while the road trip will be around fifteen days. I have contacted an agency which specializes in this and we don't have to go to Delhi to get all medical checkups done. There is a specific set of tests which if done and certified by a registered doctor would be fine. The agency will take care of everything including the Chinese Visa. All we need to do is have a valid passport with an expiry date not falling within the next six months of travel and reach Kathmandu, Nepal on our own where the agency people will receive us."

"Why is the aerial route taking almost the same time as by road?" inquired Abhiroop.

"That's because the entire route is not aerial. You still have to trek or travel in cars in some parts," clarified Abhigyan.

"What about the cost?" Abhishek was curious.

"Well, the helicopter trip will cost around 1.8 lakhs per head while the road trip will be around 1 lakh all inclusive."

Abhigyan's elder brothers had nothing more to discuss. They sat there on the sofa looking down at the floor with their face getting darker every minute. He could make out in an instant that this would yet again see the same fate the unsold controversial mansion had in the past few years. His only worry was how to go back to Ma and let her know.

"So money is the biggest road block?" Giribala Devi was sitting on the bed preparing her paan as she spoke to her three sons standing on the edge of the bed. "Are you sure there is nothing else?"

"What else can there be Ma other than the fact that this is not the right age for you to undertake such a travel. Forget about you, I myself in my forties am unsure."

"Hmm, its fine Roop, as I had told you it's just another wish. Don't take it to heart." Giribala tried to console her eldest son. "Gyan, I know what you are thinking," she said gently holding Abhigyan's hand "My answer will always be the same.... It's all or none."

June 2012

Abhigyan had no problem in identifying the hand written placard sticking out over the head of a young Nepalese man standing at the exit of Kathmandu airport.

Mr. Abhigyan Kundu and Family

Shiva and Shiva Travels

"There we have our man," shouted Abhigyan having spotted his name and beckoning his brothers and mom towards the exit.

"Mr. Kundu?" asked the young man as Abhigyan approached him with a smiling face.

Getting a nod from him he gave a big smile showing his yellow and stained teeth, "Sir, welcome to Nepal. I am Lhakpa from Shiva and Shiva Travels. There let me help you put your luggage in the car."

As all of them sat comfortably inside the Toyota Van and it started moving slowly through the heavy traffic, Lhakpa turned his head almost one eighty degree to look back at them from the navigator seat "Welcome once again, I hope the flight was good. Today you take rest in hotel, can go a bit of shopping in evening. I come in the evening and brief you on the itinerary."

"OK, Lhakpa tell me is this vehicle going to take us to Mansarovar? "Abhiroop was incredulous.

"Haha, no Sir. This vehicle no good, Land Cruiser 4500CC is waiting for you on the other side," he confirmed.

"How had been the weather up there Lhakpa?" Abhishek was inquisitive.

"The weather very clear Sir, if this continues, you will be in luck," he smiled.

A refreshing shower and a simple lunch at the hotel helped freshen up mother and sons as they were sitting on the balcony of their room enjoying the crowded expanse of the city. They were on the sixteenth floor and could see the Himalaya on the distant horizon.

"I never thought Kathmandu would be so crowded!" commented Giribala Devi chewing her paan and observing the Lilliputians down below.

"Same here Ma, I always thought Nepal is like a heavenly abode, but this is crazy. We will be here for a day I presume. Let Lhakpa confirm. But we should most definitely see the famous places here before proceeding further," remarked Abhishek.

"May I come in Sir?" Lhakpa was at the door with his beaming yellow smile.

"Please do."

"Thank you sir, I hope the lunch was good and you have liked the hotel," he inquired. Getting a positive nod from all he continued, "OK then. I will brief you very quickly how the whole trip will look like not boring you with the details as I would hand over the printed itinerary right away. Tomorrow we will go around Kathmandu. The next day we will start after breakfast and proceed towards Nepal border to reach Nyalam at the end of the day. It would be a long day and that's where you will spend a day to acclimatize. Beyond that we will be traveling by road all day and it would be a long and arduous journey but immensely rewarding. You will not regret this ever in your life, believe me. Since it's a fourteen day long trip we will take you through one day at a time. Tomorrow as I take you through a tour of this city, my folks would get your China Visa processed. Please hand me over your medical certificates now." Lhakpa was about to exit the room with the certificates when Abhiroop asked, "When would we see Kailash?"

Lhakpa smiled and said, "If everything is on schedule then on the seventh day as we drive down from Prayang. My advice to you all would be not to look beyond a day; else you will find it difficult."

"Ma, we still have time. Let's just go around Kathmandu and fly back." Winked Abhishek.

The next day was busy as they went around the whole city, cursing the traffic and lung choking pollution. Giribala Devi had always wanted to visit the Pashupatinath temple. As they approached the crowded lane bending towards the temple, they had to walk down. Abhishek, an atheist, refused to carry on the moment he saw the crowd. "I am not going in, sorry Ma."

"Why do you have to be so opinionated all the time Abhi? It's not always about you. We are here as a group, can't you peep beyond your ego to respect other's sentiments?" Abhiroop was reprimanding his brother. Abhishek cringed and looked away.

"Its fine, Roop, don't force him. Let him be here, we will carry on," Giribala gently mentioned and continued to walk slowly towards the main gate.

"I don't understand Ma why you have to take his side always. Why did he even come on this holy trip if he is so much against God? You have pampered him Ma to make him this head strong. Coming to Lord Pashupatinath and not paying him a visit! What a sin!" Abhiroop, the eldest, himself a staunch believer in God was visibly irate.

"Calm down Roop. First I have never ever taken and neither will I take the side of any one of you. I am sure heart in heart you also know it well. Secondly, he has come to this trip not because he believes in God but because he believes in me. Maybe one day you will realize Roop, the highest form of devotion to Him lies in defying Him and unconditionally loving people around."

"Please Ma, keep your esoteric religious jargons to yourself and let me pay my devotion to the Lord in peace," he had already moved away from Giribala who kept on walking slowly holding Abhigyan's hand. In all this exchange of dialog and opinions Abhigyan was the one who never ever uttered a word. Reserved, poignant and apathetic towards this world, he was the last man to be judgmental.

Next morning post breakfast as they all boarded the Toyota Van to begin their journey to Kailash; it was not even seven in the morning. It would be a long journey and we would also have to complete the immigration formalities across the border, so an early start is always advisable, Lhakpa said.

Thus began an epic journey of Giribala Devi and her sons towards her childhood dream of touching the heavenly abode. As the van heavy with the luggage and expectation started moving towards Kodari, the frontier town of Nepal, Abhiroop touched his forehead with his two hands closed and shouted: "*Har Har Mahadev*, Lord we are coming to you," as Abhishek gave a disgusted look. The drive via Dhulikhel was beautiful as they reached Kodari in no time.

"Why are we stopping?" inquired Abhigyan to Lhakpa as the van took a halt at Kodari.

"Sir, we need to get down here and cross the friendship bridge. Your Land Cruiser is waiting on the other side. We will shift your luggage, don't worry."

The brand new jet black Land Cruiser 4500 CC beast was waiting for them on the other side. Abhigyan, very fond of cars gave out an involuntary whistle as he saw it.

"Now this is what I call a machine and capable of scaling 20,000 ft," as he smiled and jumped onto the seat.

"Sir we will be now heading towards Zhangmu. Situated about 145 km from Kathmandu, at a height of 2300 m it is the main entrance point of Tibet, China. From here onwards we will be gradually gaining height and you might start feeling some discomfort. Don't hesitate to inform me immediately. The air gets rarified as we move up and due to lack of vegetation it sometimes gets difficult to breathe," Lhakpa informed.

"Ma, are you doing OK?" asked Abhiroop after they had traveled for half an hour. Giribala seemed to be having some problem breathing.

"I am fine Roop, I will let you know if I need some assistance. I think we should be reaching Zhangmu in another thirty minutes or so."

As they reached Zhangmu, Lhakpa jumped out of the car and proceeded towards the immigration office to get the formalities done. It took about half an hour to clear the immigration formalities. All three brothers were equally surprised at the efficiency of the people.

"Sir, I will take your leave from here. This is Denpa who will be taking you through the rest of the journey. I will meet you again in two weeks' time. All the best Sirs, may your wish of paying homage to the Lord come true," Lhakpa gave his characteristic smile and introduced them to their exceedingly short Tibetan guide. Denpa had a weather bitten face with a trillion wrinkles and permanently closed eyes accentuated with an eternal grin. From his physique he looked in his twenties, but his facial appearance crossed a century. How old could he be? Giribala thought as she contemplated asking but withheld herself fearing it would not be appropriate. Later maybe, she thought.

"Welcome Sir, I will be there with you through the entire journey till we come back. We will be now climbing almost 1500 m in the next three hours to reach Nyalam. The path is circuitous and some of you might feel discomfort, please let me know if you feel so."

As their black beast started climbing up the winding roads in full throttle and four gears, Abhigyan was lost in the beauty of the nature. The turquoise blue sky and the barren topography were vividly separated by the snowcapped mountains. Each breath he took made him feel ten years younger. All his office and family related tensions seemed to have thinned along with the altitude and serenity. He had put his face outside the window to let the cold air hit his face when he felt his mom's hand touch his arm gently. Yes, he knew she would be enjoying every moment of it. He turned back to see his Dada fiddling with his mobile, checking for connectivity. "Dada, why don't you switch it off and keep it away? Detach yourself from your mundane existence and take a plunge. Believe me this opportunity will never ever come to us."

"Don't advise me. Who is the elder here? Your sister-in-law needs to be informed, she must be worried," Abhiroop barked.

"Why don't you ask the Chinese Government to put up a tower on Mt. Kailash, Dada especially for you? You can even suggest the tower to be shaped like a Trishul," Abhigyan mocked jokingly.

"Gyan, don't mock your brother," Giribala reprimanded him.

"Ma, ask him to mind his own business. I am telling you he will get a slap from me one day. Don't protect him always," Abhiroop was furious. But his anger was abruptly doused by a demonic sound and some watery stuff falling on his lap. Abhishek, unable to sustain the altitude change and winding road had vomited on his brother.

"What the..." Abhiroop shouted as he tried to jump away from his brother.

Denpa, having dealt with similar situations since the last hundred years, immediately asked the driver to pull over the car as they all got out. As Abhiroop was desperately trying to clean himself with some tissue paper and water, Abhishek was still holding his head and trying to vomit. Giribala Devi patted him on the back, "Have some water Abhi, its fine. This happens with many people as we climb up. Here have some water."

"Could you not have asked the driver to stop or put your face outside the window and throw? Are you a kid? This is ridiculous. I know you did it on purpose!" Abhiroop was shouting uncontrollably.

"Dada, I am sorry. I could not control myself. It came all of a sudden. Why will I vomit on you intentionally?" Abhishek was surprised and hurt.

"Sons, don't start a fight here now. Roop control yourself, he is in pain."

After taking some rest for about fifteen minutes, as Abhishek felt better they got back into the car. Abhiroop was now sitting with Giribala Devi in the middle as the two younger brothers hopped back at the rear seats. "You know what Mejda? You have saved the Chinese Government a heavy cost of building one tower on Kailash," Abhigyan remarked pointing towards their Dada's soiled mobile phone. Abhiroop turned back and gave them a burning look as they hid their face and started to giggle.

When they reached Nyalam it was late afternoon. The accommodation at the hotel was very basic but hygienic. Giribala Devi and her eldest son were in one room while the other two brothers were in another. After freshening up and changing Abhishek was feeling a bit better as Denpa knocked at the door.

"Sir, are you feeling okay now?" he asked Abhishek.

"Yes, much better thanks Denpa. Unfortunately, I have this altitude sickness since childhood. Not having gone to the hills for many years I thought I had come over it. How will I manage the entire journey Denpa? This is just the tip of the iceberg," he was skeptical.

"Don't worry sir. We will figure out a way. Nyalam is situated at 3600m which is more than 12,000 ft. We are staying here doing nothing tomorrow to get our bodies acclimatize. I am sure you will be fine as we proceed," assured the centurion.

"Why did you have to be so rude to Abhi yesterday?" Giribala Devi was sitting on the bed after having their lunch preparing her paan. She was carrying her stock of beetle leaves hoping they won't go bad in this cold.

"Why couldn't he just stick his dumb head out and not throw it on me?" Abhiroop replied.

"Do you remember Roop when we all went together to Darjeeling? You were to appear for your board exams next year, must have been fifteen then. Abhi was hardly ten and Gyan was a toddler. Your dad, like always was driving in the hills when Abhi started to have the altitude sickness and threw up on you. Your dad was furious as he stopped the car and started shouting at him. Even I had lost my cool and was wondering why he didn't warn us beforehand?" Giribala looked up to see her son sitting quietly next to the bed, heads down, listening. "You know what you did Roop? To our surprise you shouted at dad asking him to be more considerate. He is a small kid, it's not deliberate you said and changed his clothes yourself. Just a couple of decades Roop and look where we are! Where did all that love go? What happened on the way? Was it me who failed somewhere? What has made all three of you so estranged?"

"Life has moved on Ma and so have we," replied Abhiroop as he slowly walked out of the room. Giribala sighed and looked out of the window. The small town of Nyalam was hustling in life as the white Himalayan range returned her a sad glance from the distant horizon. A cold gush of wind came in through the open door and hit her face. This is nothing she thought, my sons are standing on an ever colder terrain. She got up slowly to close the door. The agony in her heart was much more than the pain in her old bones.

"Abhi you sit on the front seat just next to the driver. Denpa, jump in at the back with me," Abhiroop declared unceremoniously and quite hurriedly as they were about to get into the Land Cruiser next morning.

"Why Dada?" Abhishek gave his brother a surprised look.

"Do you have to question everything? Do as I say. Today will be a long drive of close to seven hours and we would be scaling another 1000m as we reach Saga. You sitting on the front seat will help your giddiness. Keep on looking at the road and keep on munching on these," he said as he handed him over a packet full of chewing gums and chocolates."

"Thanks Dada."

"Don't thank me. I am doing it for myself. I am not carrying so many spare clothes. This way I will be standing next to Lord Shiva in my underwear. Now get moving, we don't have much time."

Abhiroop avoided eye contact with his mom as she smiled and looked outside the window. Abhigyan was still giggling imagining his eldest brother clad in his underwear, all ash smeared patrolling Mt. Kailash as Lord's personal bodyguard.

The journey was like a never ending one but the view was fascinating. The snowcapped mountains touched the crystal blue sky as they passed through many villages and camps of

Yak herders. The Himalayan ranges from Gaurishanker and Shishapangma showed themselves for the first time. When they reached Lalung La Pass at a height of 5000 m Abhishek shouted, "Denpa, I need a break."

"All well Abhi?" inquired Abhiroop.

"Absolutely Dada, thanks for your advice, I feel like a man born yesterday. I wanted a break to enjoy this beauty Dada, just look around, and its heaven!!!"

The whole expanse of barren beauty encircled by the white range and blue sky gave a feeling that you had reached the top of the world. Not a bird to be seen, not a sound to be heard, deathly deafening silence with just the cold wind singing next to your ears. It was as if the Gods not having able to accept such raw, harsh and unclothed beauty abandoned this place to have proceeded for greener pasture.

The rest of the journey was uneventful other than them crossing the 'Yarling Tsangpo' river which is known as Brahmaputra in India. This is where they took their last break of the day as Abhigyan kept on shooting with his SLR. "Keep the battery for the whole trip. You won't be able to recharge your batteries," advised Giribala to her youngest son. She looked at the river with moist eyes imagining that the ice cold water was coming straight from where she was headed for. I am coming my Lord, I am coming....

Tired to their bones yet rejuvenated at heart when they touched Saga the twilight was about to embrace the night.

Whole of the next day was an uneventful drive to Prayang through barren territory passing many villages and camps of Yak herders with distant view of snowcapped mountain ranges. The entire journey had flat terrain and hence was much less stressful as they reached their guest house at the end of the long day. They had been traveling for days now having traversed more than 800 km and scaled four and a half thousand meters, yet no closer to seeing the holy lake or even a glimpse of Mt. Kailash. The air was getting thinner and chillier every day as each one of them showed some signs of altitude sickness. Lhakpa's wise words: "Don't look beyond a day, the trip is too long," ringed in their ears. It seemed half a century back in their head which had started to feel light. Sensing their down trending moral Denpa spoke to them in the evening while having dinner, "All your pain till now would be washed away in happiness tomorrow Sir. Just wait till you get the first glimpse of the *sarovar*."

Uncontrolled tears flowed down Giribala Devi's eyes when late in the afternoon they got the first glimpse of the magnificent blue lake at the backdrop of the white Mt. Kailash. There was pin drop silence as Abhishek pressed the shoulder of the driver sitting next to him asking him to stop at a vantage point. Even Abhigyan was so transfixed that he couldn't take out his camera. He realized his hands were shaking in excitement. They all got down from the car and stood in awe and reverence at the virgin beauty. Giribala touched the face of her sons with her hand and whispered, "Thanks, I am grateful to have sons like you who went beyond their way to help make my dream come true. God bless you my sons, may God bless you."

The halt that night was at Chui Gumpa. The arrangement was getting more and more basic with the increasing number of days. They had covered a week, had a glimpse of their mother's dream. Yet the toughest part of the entire journey had not even begun.

"Ma, are you sure you want to go through this? You wanted to see Mt. Kailash and the sarovar with your own eyes. You have done that. Why do you want to do the *parikrama* of Kailash? Beyond Tarboche, you won't have any vehicle; it has to be on foot. The entire trek is for three days and there are points when you will be touching more than 5000 m! Listen to me, don't do this. Complete the puja tomorrow, take a holy dip in the sarovar and let's head back home." Abhishek was trying to convince his mom.

Giribala Devi was lying down in the bed all wrapped up in blankets with just her face sticking out, "I know Abhi from where you are coming and I am sure you two also nurture the same sentiments. I fully understand and respect your thought process." Then there was a silence for more than a minute as her sons thought maybe she had accepted their proposal or at least pondering over it. "Have you ever observed water very closely Abhi?

"What is water to do with your Parikrama Ma?" Abhi was irritated.

"Answer me first," Giribala commanded.

"Yes I have. It is supposed to be a tasteless, odorless, colorless liquid needed by all living beings to survive," he answered with a straight face.

"Then you have not observed well my son. The most profound character of water is its flow. Come what may it will always flow from a higher level to a lower level. Nothing can stop it from doing so. It leads to disaster if you try to do so. Be it the filthy water in your Kolkata drain or this holy crystal clear water of Mansarovar, it will undoubtedly behave the same. My son, that is the religion of water which is beyond any color, caste, origin or destination. Similarly we humans are all bound to our own religion, something which guides us beyond our own consciousness, will, like, dislike, hate or love. The Nile would flow into the heart of Sahara if it has to, knowing very well it would die. My three gems, I had embarked on this journey guided by that religion of mine, the only religion I have ever practiced in life. Please don't try and stop my flow even if I have to die."

Next morning as all four of them took a dip together in the icy water of the lake and completed the puja rituals, the chillness reached their bones. Abhiroop's teeth were clattering and he was shivering uncontrollably. Denpa wrapped him up in a double coat of blanket inside the car and gave him some brandy. However, by the time they reached Darchen his condition got worse. His temperature was running higher than 100 degrees along with respiratory trouble. When Denpa got the doctor in the guest house in the evening, Abhiroop had already got into a state of delirium and talking nonsense.

"How bad is it Doctor?" Abhigyan was incredibly worried.

"It's a typical high altitude stress condition. He must have taken a dip in the cold water today morning which aggravated the stress he was carrying with him throughout the last week of travel. I am giving few medicines. Please ensure he is given all of them and apply wet cloth on the temple if the temperature shoots up beyond 103 degree. Only tomorrow can tell whether he would be able to continue on the holy path of parikrama or not."

That night surrounded by his mom and two brothers sitting just next to his bed, Abhiroop was transported to yet another world which felt like from the previous birth, a world long dead and burnt. He was floating like a cold shadow inside a room in Kolkata as a young man in his twenties was lying on the bed half unconscious in high fever. The night was as late as an early morning. A tired lady had dozed off next to the head of the man as a teenage boy diligently checked the temperature every fifteen minutes and changed the wet cloth on the temple. The boy's hands were paining, his eyelids were getting heavier every minute, yet he fought his sleep till the last...he had to save his elder brother.

Abhiroop opened his eyes in his delirium and seeing Abhishek right next to his face said, "Abhi, how come you have grown so big?"

Next morning showed a brighter day as Abhiroop had reacted miraculously to the doctor's medicines. His fever was gone but he was feeling weak and lack of breath still.

"I would not advise you to go through with the trek sir," the doctor said. "You should rest here and then drive down to Prayang to meet the group. Rest is on your own decision as I know you must have come a long way for this." With this the doctor left as Giribala stood there in pregnant silence along with her three sons.

"Ma, I think the doctor is right. You three proceed. I will rest here and then meet you at Prayang. Maybe the Lord is not that eager to meet me so close." Abhiroop's voice was drenched in sadness.

"No way Dada," shouted Abhigyan. "We stick to the code: It's all or none. We cannot leave you behind here. Supposedly something happens to you here when we are not around? No, no, we continue in our path together. You don't worry; I am still young enough to carry you on my shoulders Dada."

"Don't be impetuous Gyan. Ma, Abhi what do you say?"

"We stick to the code," both of them replied together.

"Hmm, okay then let's give it a shot together," Abhiroop said with a smile on his face.

The 13 km journey till Tarboche, the starting point of the Parikrama did not take that long. The first day of the trek was relatively easy with gentle ups and downs all along. They were all walking very slowly and letting other pilgrims pass by. The last thing they wanted was exerting more stress on Abhiroop. To everyone's pleasure he carried himself quite well all day as they reached Dirapuk at an altitude of 4860 m. The stay was in a very basic camp in the grassy meadows overlooking the North-West face of Mt. Kailash. In the night after dinner as all three brothers came out of the camp the view fascinated them. The moonlight had fallen on the crest of Mt. Kailash as the myriad diamonds bejeweled the sky like a newlywed bride. The dazzling sword hanging from the belt of Orion seemed to have surgically cut them from the materialistic world back in Kolkata, a world which seemed so fake, superficial and meaningless. The only sound heard in that frozen bliss was the heavy sigh of the three brothers as they exchanged a tacit glance and went back to the tent.

The next day trek proved to be the most difficult part. The journey was uphill as they had to reach Drolma La at 5200 m, the highest point of the trek. Abhiroop had started to develop heavy breathing while Giribala Devi and Abhishek were both struggling badly. Their entire body was going numb as Denpa kept on motivating them and pushing them along. As they finally reached Drolma La, heaving a sigh of relief hoping the worst was over something unexpected happened. Abhigyan too overwhelmed with the serene beauty and unable to control his excitement taking photographs did not notice a loose rock and slipped down one side of the mountain path. The fall was about 6 ft., not deep enough to be fatal but enough to twist his ankle badly. By the time he limped his way to Zuthulphuk, the end of the trek for that day, his swelling had become quite bad.

"How is it Gyan?" asked Abhiroop holding his brothers leg gently trying to gauge the damage.

"Looks bad Dada. Not sure how I can pull through the last day," he replied.

"So much to your carrying me on your shoulders Hercules," Abhiroop joked and winked. "Don't worry. Take the medicine the doctor has given, have the bandage on. We will all pull through together tomorrow. Have a pain killer and try and have a good night sleep."

The last and the eleventh day trek of 10 km to Prayang made Giribala Devi cry. It was not the physical pain but the tears of joy as Abhiroop and Abhishek took turns to pull Gyan along as he held the long end of a stick trying to limp forward. She knew her obstinacy of sticking to the code from the very first day had not gone in vain. Farsighted Giribala knew very well that sitting at the heart of Kolkata, she alone could never mend the crack. It needed something larger than life to bring them back.

"There is one last request I have my sons," Giribala Devi was sitting next to a fire at a camp in Prayang. "If you could ask Denpa to take us back to Mansarovar tomorrow in the morning before proceeding back? I want to take one last dip. I know it would be a bit out of the way, but since we have the car all to ourselves, he should not have a problem."

"Whatever you wish ma."

The early morning sun had smeared golden dust on the divine waters of the lake adding its sheen, the frozen tip of Mt. Kailash was yet to rise from its slumber when Giribala Devi entered the freezing water of the lake. Her three sons held her hand, knee deep in the water, looking at her with moist eyes.

"So this is it, Ma?"

"Yes my gems. This is it. I was, am and would always be proud to have got sons like you. Promise me you will always be next to each other as you have been in the last few days. Remember, my peace is with you three, no one else. My religion had led me to this confluence dear, now it is up to you where you want me to go."

With this she slowly started walking towards Kailash with her palm closed and eyes beyond the horizon, deeper and deeper into the water. She never turned back. When finally she disappeared, the three brothers were holding each other and were in tears. Their Ma was gone. All that floated around them on the water was ashes, her last sign.

They gave a long last look at Kailash, hugged each other and turned back towards the car with Gyan holding the empty urn. The return journey would be a long one. It would be lighter by weight but heavier in heart.